THE GINGERBREAD CAFÉ

A HOCKEY SWEETHEART NOVEL

JEAN ORAM

The Gingerbread Café
by Jean Oram
Copyright © 2022 Jean Oram
All rights reserved.
First Edition

Printed in the United States of America unless otherwise stated on the last page of this book. Published by Oram Productions Alberta, Canada.

COMPLETE LIBRARY OF CONGRESS CATALOGING-IN-PUBLICATION DATA AVAILABLE ONLINE

Oram, Jean.

The Gingerbread Café / Jean Oram.—1st. ed.

ISBN: 978-1-989359-91-4, 978-1-990833-73-1, 978-1-990833-74-8, 978-1-989359-90-7, 978-1-990833-95-3 (large print)

Ebook ISBN: 978-1-989359-69-3

First Oram Productions Edition: April 2025

Front cover design by Jess Mastorakos

For Marjory Jean who completed her journey here on earth the same day I completed Miranda's story. May your legacy continue.

The Gingerbread Café

———

*M*iranda wondered if coming here was self-protection or self-sabotage. Either way, it was clear she wasn't ready to date again.

She'd come to a cute sports café her colleague Daisy-Mae Ray had told her about, thinking she might find a man who liked similar things.

But it was Wednesday.

Two o'clock, to be specific. That was hardly prime man-finding time if you were on the prowl.

She sighed and took a stool at the café's back bar. The sports-themed sitting area was empty with the exception of one balding man dunking a well-decorated gingerbread man into his beer. Miranda cringed to think what *that* might taste like.

The Gingerbread Café had a unique vibe. Part sports pub, part coffee shop. A few antique coffee grinders sat on shelves hung between screens set to sports channels, and the chalkboard menus offered everything from fancy lattes to local brews. The long wood slab that served as a back bar had a covered cake platter to her right, loaded with stacks of beautifully decorated cookies. Beyond that was a basket with bags of flavored bar nuts: hickory, hot and spicy, smoked mustard…

The building, however, smelled like a heavenly bakery. A mix of gingerbread, roasted coffee beans, baked sugar, and butter.

A great place for coffee on a Wednesday. Or an early afternoon beer while you waited for the evening's local band to play on the mini stage set in the corner, as advertised by the poster on the door.

Not such a great place to pick up a "sports-minded" man unless you were looking for a day-drinker.

This wasn't where she'd find the kind of man she could take to her parents' Sunday dinners in their ten-bedroom mansion. Not that she often went to those dinners. But still. She should at least try, right?

She took in the wall to her left. A weathered wooden sign that said beer would be free tomorrow, and beside it hung a shadow box holding a signed hockey puck.

Hockey.

She sighed.

She'd never noticed how ever-present the sport was until she'd bought herself an NHL team several months ago.

She smoothed her hands over the long, smooth maple coffee bar. The tree must have been close to one hundred years old before it had been turned into a bar here in San Antonio.

She craned her neck, on the lookout for the barista/bartender.

Maybe all of this was a sign she should go back to the office.

Except she'd actually tried today. Tried to do the "normal" thing in hopes of snagging interest from a regular, come-as-you-are kind of man. She'd forgone her usual jewelry and perfect makeup that went with the slays-all-day-as-some-big-boss-woman-you-should-be-afraid-of wardrobe she donned in order to be taken seriously in the very male-dominated world of hockey. By all appearances, this afternoon, she was just a normal woman. She was wearing an old sweatshirt from Brown, jeans from the department store, barely there makeup, and her beautifully cut black hair was tucked in a ponytail. In other words, Weekend Miranda.

She didn't look like a woman who owned an NHL team.

She winced and peered at the large TV in the corner. At least she wasn't on the screen at the moment, being raked over the coals by a sportscaster. The instant the station started talking about the start of the hockey season, though, she'd be up there in her Slays All Day getup, and her cover as a normal person would be completely blown.

The networks loved to predict her downfall and spent hours analyzing how she worked with her managers to run the team, her input on player trading decisions, her involvement with the players—not romantically, but of course there was plenty of speculation there. They seemed to assume that any less-than-predictable business moves made by her were mistakes, not that she had a multi-year strategy in mind and was working toward building a legacy for her late grandfather, who'd once played in the league.

The sports networks expected her to bat her lashes, giggle, and throw money at her team's problems. She didn't do the first two, but she was a tad guilty of the third. Buying an expansion team that was ready to fold in its second season came with a lot of financial issues. She'd known that going in but had hoped to turn things around a bit faster and for nobody to notice her work.

Then again, marching into interviews to defend her team's captain, Maverick Blades, as the press continued to slam him with some pretty nasty speculation about what happened on his last team, had maybe brought a little extra attention her way.

Coming to this café to find true love before her ovaries turned to dust was a mistake. She couldn't pretend to be someone else in here. She needed a Plan B. Maybe she could convince some nice man online that she was just an average gal with an average office job. Then once they had fallen in love, she could reveal who she really was. It worked in the movies. Why not in real life?

"Sorry, I didn't realize you'd come in," a barista said, coming from the direction of the restrooms, carting a mop. He was about her age, approaching his mid-thirties, and wore a backward ball cap. He looked rugged, handsome, strong and sporty, despite the crisp white dress shirt that somehow accommodated his broad shoulders. A bit of stubble like he hadn't shaved for a day and a half darkened his jaw, and his eyes were dark, with lashes long enough they ought to be a crime on anyone who didn't care about mascara.

He leaned the mop against the wall before moving behind the bar. "What can I get you?"

His sleeves were rolled up to his elbows, displaying cords of muscles. He placed his hands on the bar, his index finger finding the slight indent from one of the old tree's knots, like an unconscious habit. He had wide hands. The kind that would leave you feeling safe and protected with just a simple touch to your lower back while guiding you through crowds, ensuring you didn't get separated. He seemed like the type of guy who'd do that. Even though he knew you could take care of yourself. He'd act like you were a team, in it together.

His skin was bronzed, and he probably always looked good, healthy. Even in the dead of winter.

"Don't worry, I washed them."

"What's that?" she asked, glancing up at him. My, he was handsome.

"My hands." He lifted them, showing her. A ring on his left. Of course. She nearly slouched again.

No, that was her left, his right. The ring was big, manly, and it looked like it might be a championship ring of some sort. Before she could determine what it was, he tucked his hands in his jeans pockets. He was built like an athlete. All muscles and completely hot.

He wasn't out of place here. In fact, the antique coffee grinder and beautiful gingerbread cookies were out of place. Not him.

"I like your bar topper. Maple?" She ran her hands down the flat expanse of cool wood.

"I had it shipped down from my parents' maple syrup farm in Quebec."

"Quebec? I don't hear a French accent."

"Yeah, no? You don't hear it, eh?" he said, putting on a thick accent.

"I do now for some reason."

That earned her a grin that made her stomach flip.

She hooked her feet on the stool's rail and pushed herself up, leaning over the edge of the bar. She'd noticed on the chalkboard menu above her that the café was licensed, and it felt like it might be five o'clock somewhere in the world.

"Can I get…?" She eyed his stock of drink garnishes. It was impressive, and it tipped her decision firmly away from one of the warm pumpkin spice drinks listed on the specials board. "Something with a wedge of orange and a cherry?"

"Missed lunch? Our gingerbread banana bread is to die for."

She shook her head. She would never miss a meal. But a drink with a few stackable garnishes sounded delicious.

The bartender was studying her, his arms braced on the bar. Those wide shoulders of his. He looked like a defenseman for one of the N and Ls of the sporting world. NHL or NFL. Too bad she didn't date players.

Although both sports were in-season, meaning there was no way the man would have the time—or the inclination—to work what was likely a minimum wage food service job.

"Because if you like snacks with your drinks, my Caesars are a meal as well as a work of art. Pickle, bacon, cherry tomato, deep fried onion, and a tiny square of focaccia."

"Seriously? What is that? A salad?"

"A bartender never jokes about his drinks."

"I thought you were a barista."

"What matters is that I make the best Caesar in town." He pointed to a plaque hanging near the cash register. She was too far away to read it but guessed it was evidence of his claim.

"I don't know what a Caesar is."

"It's kind of like a Bloody Mary. And then I go overboard with the garnishes."

"Sure, I'll give it a try."

"You won't be disappointed."

"Can I make it a virgin?" She might still try to squeeze some work in later tonight, and she wanted to be clear-headed.

The bartender looked slightly pained by her request, but nodded.

"And not too spicy, thanks."

"Trust me," he said, not too patiently, "and let me make the drink."

A competitive, all-for-the-art barista/bartender who looked like he could prevent a professional athlete from getting past him. Yeah, she was intrigued.

And not just because she was tired of the personality-contorting silver spoon types she'd grown up around—and her mother kept trying to match her with. She simply wanted someone genuine. Someone who paused to feel things. Someone who would consider her, who wouldn't shush her or treat her like an ornament. Someone who would be home to feed the cat for her.

Not that she had a cat. But with the right man, she could have one without worrying about it starving.

She moved her hands over the glossy-coated maple. "That must've been expensive, having this shipped all the way to San Antonio."

The wood bar looked like it ran, unbroken, for a full twenty feet.

The bartender remained quiet as he fixed her drink. His moves were efficient, methodical. Soon he set the drink in front of her.

"Wow. This is a masterpiece." The stick of speared snacks was artfully arranged. And the glass had been flawlessly rimmed with what looked like a variety of spices. She pulled out her phone and took a photo.

"Instagram worthy?" he asked.

"No, I have to send this to my sister. She always finds the

prettiest drinks in town. It'll kill her not knowing where I had this."

"Ah, sibling rivalry. It's not just for kids anymore."

"I have to take the wins where I can with my family."

He chuckled but didn't ask. She liked him all the more for it. Especially since she felt guilty. Her sister Deanna was the only one in the family that seemed to half-understand her, and she'd spent a lot of her own social currency defending Miranda and her life choices lately.

He waited for her to remove the stick of garnishes and take a sip. "Well?" He crossed his arms, his grin confident as she savored the flavor. "It's the best, right?"

It was. Not too spicy and definitely delicious. She gave an indifferent lift of her shoulder. "Looks better than it tastes."

He huffed in disbelief. "You're a liar. This is the best Caesar you've ever had."

She gasped. "I can't believe you call your customers liars!"

He shrugged. Casual, confident, comfortable. But not too cocky or arrogant. He knew exactly where he stood in the world, and he owned it. This man tickled her insides.

She took another sip, unable to resist the drink. It was shocking the café wasn't filled to the rafters with customers if his other drinks were as good as this one. The room was scented with wonderful baking, too. Scents didn't lie.

"It kills you to admit that this is the best Caesar you've ever tasted, doesn't it?" He was leaning on the bar, his voice low. She had a feeling that this man, with the dark, dark eyes, enjoyed being right and winning as much as she did.

She took another sip, half of the drink already gone. "More than I'll ever admit."

"I'll take that as a win." He slid her a napkin for the stick of snacks she was still holding, and she set down the garnishes.

Maybe it was the tabasco from the Caesar warming her stomach, but it felt good flirting with him.

He ran a hand over the wood that separated them. "My brother was coming down for a visit, and he threw this on top of his holiday trailer. The whole counter cost me nothing more than a couple of drinks and filling his hollow leg for a few days."

"Sounds worth it."

He gave the room thoughtful consideration. His expression suggested he felt as though the café should mean something more. Kind of like when she'd been granted access to her trust account years ago. It meant nothing to her until she found something meaningful to put it toward—the team and her grandfather's memory. She was fulfilling a dream he'd never been able to fulfill for himself.

"What made you move so far away from your family?" she asked.

"Work. Then when I was changing careers, a buddy found this space, and it was perfect. Great location. Decent price. And I like San Antonio. So I stayed."

She nodded, thinking. He was a long way from his family. While she didn't mind a little distance between her and the overbearing ways of her parents, she was still only across the city. Not in a whole different country.

"Big family?" she asked.

"A brother and a sister. You?"

"Two sisters. Are you French Catholic?" Now that he'd pointed out where he was from, she could hear a hint of a Canadian French accent, particularly when he spoke of his family.

He smiled. "Somewhere back in the family tree. We haven't been practicing for a generation or two. Are you?"

"Catholic? No. My family believes and worships—" She caught herself before the adage slipped off her tongue. Her family believed and worshipped money. All hail the mighty dollar. It was the most important thing. That and image. They were competitive, but loathe to admit it, and would frequently shame her when she was too blatantly competitive. Apparently, it wasn't ladylike, and she'd never find a man acting like that.

So far, it appeared to be true.

"They worship work?" the bartender prompted.

She shook her head. She wasn't going there. She pulled a piece of bacon off the garnish stick and mindlessly chewed it. Yeah, it would add to her curves—she'd long ago forfeited a spot in the skinniest woman at the country club competition. Quite happily. Life was for enjoying.

And anyway, she looked good. She liked her generous, plush curves and believed she looked as a woman should.

"Too soon to tell me your deep, dark family secrets?" His eyes danced as he leaned against the counter that separated them.

She flashed a smile. "We don't even know each other's names. Of course it's too soon."

"Bartender confidentiality applies here. But if it makes you feel better..." He reached out a hand for her to shake. "My friends call me Dak."

DAK CAUGHT Miranda Fairchild's beat of hesitation before responding to his outstretched hand. He was curious if she'd tell him her real name or if she'd pretend to be someone else. Dressed casually, she was more his type than the version of herself he often saw on TV. In interviews, her clothing and impeccable makeup were like a much-needed armor against the vicious sportscasters who found fault and insanity in everything she did with and for her team.

Still, despite the difference between the two women, Dak was ninety-nine percent confident he was flirting with Miranda Fairchild, owner of the San Antonio Dragons hockey team. This woman in his café had the same thought-out certainty in the way she spoke. Although this woman had reddish streaks in her black hair. Too fine for the camera to pick up? And there were fine lines around her eyes that were faint, but not invisible. She was pretty. Both versions of her.

Finally, he released her smooth hand, realizing he'd held it a bit too long.

"And I'm a friend?" she asked, referring to his comment that his friends called him Dak.

Dakarai, a Shona name that meant happiness, wasn't common in North America. On hockey teams, it was always shortened to Dak. And he'd been on teams so long the only person who still called him Dakarai was his mother.

"You're a friend if you tell me your name."

"Miranda." *Knew it.* "But my friends call me She Who Slays All Day."

Dak laughed. He bet the nickname fit her to a tee.

She gave a pert little smile that bordered on mischievous.

"Yeah?"

"Yeah," she replied.

Miranda Fairchild was flirting with him. If her drink wasn't a virgin, he'd blame it on the Caesar because she didn't come across as flirty on TV. She was much more the slayer nickname with her professional, quick briefs that were to the point and lacking in apologies or explanations for her unorthodox ways. It had almost made him want to rejoin the NHL just to be on her team.

"And how did you earn that mouthful of a nickname?" he asked, leaning against the counter.

"It's a secret."

Was she being coy? Or was she intentionally hiding her identity?

Whatever she was doing, she was definitely flirting with that sweet smile that bordered on unexpected shyness.

It was cute. It wasn't the smooth, calculated game some women played.

But Miranda Fairchild shy? That didn't seem possible. Maybe she had a twin sister.

Then again, he was pretty sure a woman who took so much public flak had to have earned some insecurities and reservations. That could account for some real-life shyness when she was without the on-screen armor.

"Another secret?" he asked gently.

She nodded and sipped her drink.

"You seem to have a lot of those."

"Don't worry, I've earned them all." She set down the glass, the full force of her gaze striking him. There was nothing extraordinary about her eyes. They weren't a unique shape or an unusual color, and yet there was a depth behind them that caught him, hooked him, made him feel things he didn't want to.

And definitely not for the owner of the local NHL team. He'd left that life behind almost a year ago with no plans of returning.

"You can earn secrets?" he asked.

"Definitely."

In his periphery, he noticed Kirk coming closer, his empty

beer stein in hand. The man weaved once, then stumbled, crashing into Miranda as he tried to place his glass on the bar.

"Oh! Are you okay?" Miranda jumped up, steadying him with a concerned expression.

"Just a whoopsy," Kirk said.

Miranda laughed amicably at his large, sloppy grin and took her seat again. "Glad you're okay."

Dak placed Kirk's tab on the counter as a hint that he was cut off. The man nodded deeply and opened his wallet, paying slowly with one-dollar bills, creating a careful pile.

"And one extra for you, my dear friend," Kirk said, placing a bill beside the stack he'd created.

"Thank you, kind sir," Dak said, placing the bills in the cash register at the end of the bar and his tip in the tip jar.

The man saluted Dak and meandered toward the exit.

"Is he okay to get home?" Miranda asked.

"Kirk lives in the apartment above the store next door."

"Oh. Good."

Dak considered Miranda again. He didn't get the vibe that she was a train wreck or looking for ways to upset the NHL's boys' club like the press had suggested on many occasions.

And he hated it.

Absolutely hated it because it meant he might have to give his buddy Maverick Blades, and the job opportunity he'd told him about, honest consideration. Even if it was for the worst-ranked team with the poorest reputation in the entire league. A team where the owner took in battered players nobody else wanted as though she was running a rescue shelter.

Miranda's team.

Because this woman might just be trying to put some good things out into the world, and he'd be a royal jerk if he ghosted the interview.

Then again, he was pretty sure her team's new charity was just a much-needed tax break and a way for her players to look good somewhere, if not on the ice.

He could ghost it. Keep himself away from the NHL while he continued to lick his wounds.

He should have stayed in bed today. Understanding, or empathizing with, this woman wasn't going to lead to anything good, because he was happy with his new life. Sure, he was still adjusting. But his new café was winning awards, and it got busy during rush times. What was there not to love?

"Do you have any pets?" Miranda asked.

"Sorry?"

"Pets?"

"Yeah, a dog. You?"

"Even better than a cat," she said, mostly to herself.

"How's that?"

"Married?" she asked.

"No. Are you?"

"Who takes care of the dog while you're here?"

He crossed his arms, resting his forearms along the bar's edge, putting him closer to eye level with her. "I hire a dog walker."

"Oh."

"You don't have a dog, I take it?"

She shook her head.

"Tried and failed?"

"Worst gift ever. He ate my couch. I tried taking him to work. He ate my desk."

He smirked. It had likely been a very expensive desk.

"And you gave up?" Sure, he'd only just met Miranda, but it didn't seem like her to give up on something.

"Sometimes you have to cut your losses early on."

"And?"

She smiled, an open, sunny one that hit him in the gut. "My ex now has the evil hound."

Dak let out a bark of laughter at her joyful proclamation. "Well worth giving up in that case."

"I'm not home enough to be a proper pet owner," she said, picking at her shirt where it clung close to her midriff, "and there's nobody in my life who takes care of me or my stuff. Especially not something as consistently needy as a pet." She blinked. "Oh, wow. I sound bitter."

"Let me guess. You're a Type A, run-your-own-empire kind of chick?" He took in her outfit, hoping she'd fess up to her true identity. Then he could let it slip that he was someone she might know, too. Or soon would. If he got the job.

She smoothed her ponytail. "Yeah. Something like that."

She wasn't going to reveal who she was. Fair enough. The lack of trust stung a bit though. Then again, she was a woman in his café at two in the afternoon, midweek. She had problems. Maybe even more than the press had already aired.

"Slays all day." He smiled sadly and shook his head. "Not my type. Too high maintenance. Can't even take care of a dog."

"It's too bad." She gave him a put-on forlorn look.

He waited, unsure where she was going but certain she was flirting. "Why's that?" he finally asked.

"I bet you could keep up." There was that shy smile again.

He laughed. It felt good to have a woman bust his ribs. Not just to break up a quiet Wednesday afternoon before the three o'clock coffee rush, but because somehow, flirting and laughing with her was like coming out of the depths. Like standing in a ray of warmth and much-needed sunshine.

He hadn't had many moments like that since retirement, even with throwing himself into the Gingerbread Café, which was supposed to be a fulfilling dream.

"I don't know about that, dragon slayer."

Her good mood fell along with her smile at the mention of her team's name. Her head tipped down as she wiped a few crumbs off the bar in front of her.

He should admit he had an interview next week with the Dragons' Children's Charity.

Although it was possible that she already knew and was checking him out on his own turf. Few owners would do that, but Miranda was a lot more hands-on than most. By the sounds of it, she was in the thick of it with her various managers, weighing in on everything from trades to branding strategies.

And yet, she wasn't acting like Ms. Slays All Day or probing him about his life—other than the pets thing. She was flirting with him like she didn't have a clue who he was.

It was true that he'd never been a big name in the NHL despite his solid career. He'd had plenty of fans but wasn't an attention junkie by any means—especially during his final years.

And somehow, getting to know Miranda without expectations or any prior knowledge to get in their way...he liked it. He liked the realness of their moments and the realness of Miranda Fairchild.

But he really hoped her being here and making him laugh wasn't some kind of sign.

Miranda was a lot more curious about the bartender than she

expected to be. Well, pub owner. Café owner? It was clear he owned the place.

Dak moved down the bar and she tried not to act disappointed. He made her feel like she was an ace at flirting. It was fun and felt exciting. She didn't want his focus on her to end. And it wasn't just acknowledgment; he truly focused on her, and it was intense and thrilling. It was as though he saw a part of her he liked—a part she hadn't even realized existed it was so average and ordinary to her.

She should have shed her office warrior wardrobe and done this 'normal' act a long time ago.

Dak came back with a small bowl of nuts, setting them in front of her, then rolling his right shoulder like he had a pinched muscle. "Fastest shelling is twenty seconds. You beat that time and your drink is free."

Miranda studied the bowl of peanuts. "Aren't you worried about someone having an anaphylactic reaction?" She'd thought peanuts were all but banned in most places these days.

"There's a sign on the door."

"A peanut warning?"

"It says: Don't die in here."

She smirked. "I'm sure that works brilliantly."

"So far, I'm batting a thousand."

She wiped her hands on her jeans, studying the nuts. "Twenty seconds, huh?"

She glanced up at Dak, then away, that annoying bout of shyness she kept experiencing around him taking over again. She felt like a twelve-year-old whose crush had just said hi to her for the first time.

"Well? You in?" Dak asked. He quirked his brows at her, and she gripped the edges of her stool so she didn't do something stupid like launch herself over the bar and kiss those mesmerizing lips of his.

She focused on the peanuts. There wasn't enough time to shell them individually and beat the record. She could feel Dak watching her as she plotted her strategy. It was clear she was going to challenge the record. Apparently, according to her mother, it was there for all to see in her eyes and the set of her jaw once she decided she wanted something.

"Define shelled," she asked.

"No peanuts left in shells. Peanuts in bowl."

She rolled her shoulders and rocked her neck from side to side.

Dak set a cell phone on the counter with a timer app opened.

She met his eyes. "I hate losing."

"Then don't." There was something so familiar about this man. Was it simply his love of competition as well? Maybe that was all this fun spark between them was—the thrill of competition and her continually winning the game of making him smile.

She closed her eyes briefly, secretly wishing they could carry on like this for hours—two normal people having a moment on a Wednesday afternoon.

She pushed up her sleeves and nodded to Dak.

"Countdown at the ready, Miranda," he said calmly.

She loved how her name sounded in his deep voice, the way she could feel how he wanted her to beat the record.

Focus.

"Three, two..." she counted, her fingers gripping the side of the bowl. "One!" She dumped peanuts onto the counter and pushed the bottom of the bowl down on the pile of nuts, cracking the cluster of shells in several goes. Quickly she picked the nuts from the debris, dumping them into the bowl. She dusted her hands. Job complete. "What's my time?"

Dak grinned and held his phone close to his chest, refusing to show her the timer. If she didn't know any better, she would almost say he was smitten with her. Or his experience as a bartender had simply made him super affable and good at flirting. Either way, he was more fun than the rule-following robots in the country club who steadfastly refused to let her be one of the guys.

"I beat it," she said confidently. "By how much?"

"Who says you beat it?"

"I know I did. What's my time?"

"Guess."

"What do I win if I'm right?"

"Who said there's a prize?"

She gave a huff of displeasure.

"Bragging rights," he suggested.

"Make it worth it."

"Fine. A kiss."

"Funny."

Was she blushing? She felt like she was. As well as trying not to smile. Or look at his lips and imagine a kiss.

Who was the woman he turned her into?

"Okay, yeah," he said casually. "We just met. How about a lunch date instead?"

"A lunch date?" Her heart was thrumming. Dak liked her. This wasn't polite flirting in hopes of a bigger tip. He *liked* her. She wanted to text her friends and tell them this hottie had the hots for her! Competitive, unruly, bossy *her*.

"I'm intrigued by you," Dak said, and she nearly fell off her stool.

"You are?"

"I am."

They were holding eye contact for way too long. She felt like she was making promises she couldn't keep. He'd quickly learn who she was, and while she hadn't dated in almost two years, she could foresee how the press would be unrelenting in their invasion of privacy and likely even attempt to emasculate the poor man.

She looked down, swept some shells away from the edge of the counter so they wouldn't fall on the floor.

Maybe she could pretend to be normal for a little longer. Maybe he didn't like hockey and the memorabilia on the walls was for ambiance. After all, none of the channels were playing hockey game highlights.

She couldn't keep her life secret forever, but maybe for just one date. One blissful lunch where she was nothing more than a woman, laughing and flirting with a man who saw the real her beneath her career and growing reputation. And liked her.

"Why lunch?"

"I'm usually here at supper."

"Usually. But not always." There was room for a girlfriend in his life?

"True." He was watching her, that slight smile curving his sweet lips upward. "Not always."

"The café is your wife?"

"My soul's only current purpose." There was that brief twist in his expression again like he was trying to convince himself the café was it, the goal, the very thing he should be happy about. Basically, he looked like she probably did hanging out at the country club with her family's friends. Smiling, knowing she had it all, but somehow not feeling connected to it in the way she thought she should.

"So I'm not worth missing a night in a café-slash-pub for?" She narrowed her eyes, flirting, teasing. Dak laughed, stepping backward as though needing room for the giant burst of joyful sounds coming from deep within his chest.

He settled, saying kindly, "Not yet, you're not."

She gave him a disgusted look, but he returned it with a confidence she secretly adored.

"The soup kitchen wouldn't understand me blowing off my night behind their stove for a woman."

"You volunteer?"

"One night a week."

"You cook?"

"You don't?"

"Maybe I do, maybe I don't." She liked that he wouldn't bow at her feet. He was willing to push, dish back, banter and not give in.

"What's the runner-up prize if I don't guess right?" she asked, gesturing to his phone.

"You get to eat the nuts. For free."

She gazed at the mess she'd made and crinkled her nose. How clean was this bar topper? "I think I'd better win."

He laughed and swept an arm down the counter, clearing away the shells and peanut bits, dumping it onto a tray, which he then tipped over a trash can. "For the record, lunch with me is better than a bowl of nuts."

"Not everyone can say that."

"You've been here at closing time and have seen my competition, have you?"

She laughed along with him. Miranda had a feeling Dak wanted her to win that lunch date more than he'd admit.

She felt the same way.

CHAPTER 2

$\mathcal{M}$iranda locked her front door and turned to face her car, which was sitting in her new home's dirt driveway. She inhaled the fresh country air and spread her arms. She had a date with a very hunky man, and the day felt perfect.

Her parents thought she was crazy for buying a farmhouse along the edge of Sweetheart Creek. The town's population was less than 5,000, and their diner was filled with gossip. And so, yes, maybe she was a bit off her rocker for moving out here on the weekends, but she also felt like she could be her true self. Unplug. Unwind. All the stuff recommended by mental health gurus.

And it wasn't as if she'd gone into the purchase blindly. Her team's captain, Maverick Blades, had told her about the town, the kindness of the townspeople, and how he could putter about without notice while he fixed up his own little ranch house several miles from hers. The second she expressed interest in his low-key retreat, he had this home's listing up on his phone and was telling her how great it would be.

So far, even though Miranda had only been here a few weeks, he was completely correct. The small house was homey, as was the town, and the people were real, the setting quiet. She could leave the city on Friday nights when there were no home games to attend, whip off her bra, slip on her yoga pants, pour a glass of wine, and curl up on her couch in front of the fireplace and read or watch romantic comedies. She even had her own little duck pond out back under some arching oaks where she could snuggle in a sherpa blanket at dusk with a thermos of cocoa and enjoy the sunset as it left trails of colors on the water's surface.

Miranda jogged down the three steps to the grass and crossed through a small rose garden to her car. The stone path was charmingly overgrown, and a frog hopped out of her way as she moved.

Climbing into her car in a comfy pair of jeans and a sweatshirt to battle the early November chill, she smiled.

She had a date with Dak.

Just a normal guy who worked to earn a living. A man who was all about real life. Owning a dog, volunteering, running a business as well as working out and taking care of his body, judging from those powerful shoulders of his.

When Dak had begun setting up plans to claim his lunch date for Saturday, she'd mentioned she'd be out of town. He'd joked that she was trying to escape their date, and she'd quipped back that she'd be in Sweetheart Creek doing absolutely, blissfully nothing, and had he ever heard of the place?

He'd replied that he'd meet her at the Longhorn Diner at noon, Saturday.

Of course he knew Sweetheart Creek. The man seemed to

intuitively understand the things that mattered to her. How was it that everything about him already felt so right?

As Miranda backed her car into her driveway's turn-around spot, she smiled, then shot out to go meet Dak.

She tamped down her smile, reminding herself there was no point getting attached since things wouldn't last. He'd soon discover who she was, the bad press that plagued her, and go running for the Texas hills. Well, further into them than they already were here in Sweetheart Creek.

But even if they weren't destined to last—like she predicted—she could still enjoy their date.

She angle parked on Main Street between two dusty pickup trucks, right in front of the Longhorn's cute brick and wood exterior. She knew that inside she would be greeted by classic red-checkered tablecloths, a row of booths along one wall, and a row of stools set along the back counter. The diner was darling for the way it seemed stuck in time.

Miranda scanned the vehicles parked out front, trying to guess if any of them were Dak's. Unless he drove a truck, she was the first to arrive.

She pushed open the glass door with its Go Tornadoes football sign stuck to it, immediately checking for Dak. He would be easy to spot with his large build, and, likely, a herd of flirting women surrounding him. He was the hottest man she'd met in ages—and she'd met plenty. But it wasn't just his appearance that sparked her. She loved being able to release her fiery side without him giving her a side-eyed warning glance, hissing at her to cool it.

If she wasn't careful, she'd find herself in too deep, proposing they run away to some country nobody had ever heard of. They'd stick their toes in the sand and just be their real selves all day long without interference from the outside world. Laughing and kissing...

Despite the fleeting thought that her heart would be safer if she stood up Dak, she inhaled the scent of garlic and butter and found an empty table near the front.

She scanned the room again in case she'd missed him. Plenty of cowboy hats and gorgeous big hair, but no golden-skinned man. At the back, a TV screen, new since the last time she'd been in, had drawn a group of men talking football.

Another thing to like about Sweetheart Creek: it was a football town, not a hockey town. So while she was certain she was the subject of gossip here, it had less to do with hockey and more to do with whose house she'd bought and whether she planned to make changes to it.

Across the room, locals Violet and Daisy-Mae, both Dragons employees, smiled and waved her over just as the door opened and Dak came in. Miranda tipped her head toward the man to suggest she was meeting with him, and the two women swung their heads out of their booth to take a gander.

Daisy-Mae, a cute, buckle bunny kind of woman who might often be found at rodeos, grinned and mouthed, "Hot!"

Miranda gave a tiny nod as a shot of pleasure rocketed through her at the truth of Daisy-Mae's statement.

She swore she heard Daisy-Mae squeal in excitement on Miranda's behalf. In appearance, Daisy-Mae was her total opposite. Sunny yellow hair versus Miranda's black. Slim versus not-so-slim. Down-home buckle bunny versus slays all day.

As different as they appeared, Daisy-Mae, with her honest sincerity and smarts, was willing to cause a stir when something mattered to her. Within a week of starting with the team, she'd become part of Miranda's trusted inner circle after defending the team captain and taking on the Dragons' publicity duo over some ridiculous ideas.

Miranda focused on Dak as he walked her way, their eyes meeting as he spotted her. She allowed her gaze to lock on his, holding it for longer than she should. The man moved smoothly and with confidence as he took up the ground between them. His large, warm hand paused briefly on her shoulder, and she blinked, surprised at the contact. He placed a kiss on her cheek, bringing with him the scent of gingerbread. The man was delicious in every way.

"Waiting long?" he asked, while she still swooned over his cheek-kissing manners.

"Just got here."

She resettled herself, running her tongue over her front teeth to ensure her freshly applied lipstick wasn't smeared. Suddenly, she wanted to look good. She'd carefully chosen her outfit, leaning toward very casual. But now she felt as though she'd dressed wrong, that her appearance was too lacking in care, as though she felt Dak wasn't important enough to put in the effort.

He sat across from her with a soft, "Hi."

"Hi."

She had a moment of uncertainty about what she was doing here. He wasn't her flirty bartender now. He was her date. A man being considered for his potential.

Which meant so was she.

Daisy-Mae shot Miranda another smile while she craned to take a better look at Dak. He was wearing a navy button-up shirt that brought out the darkness of his skin, his eyes, his hair. He was handsome. His shirt was sharp, not cheap. Impeccably pressed and cut to accommodate his wide shoulders. Even his curly hair was cut perfectly. His look wasn't achieved with coupons or careful shopping. Money was behind it.

Maybe he was a good businessman and used what little money he earned to look good. That wasn't a crime. It didn't mean he was similar to the men at the country club and that he'd expect her to look a certain way as well.

Oh, she was lost. So lost. She wanted Dak to be different.

She'd lifted her menu to hide behind while she pulled herself together, and now she peeked over it to find him staring at her. He was taking in every detail, like she was desirable in her jeans and sweatshirt. Attractive despite the lack of apparent money, family connections, or the right outfit. He was looking at her as though she was someone who could weaken his knees. Like she was someone who mattered.

Oh, trouble, trouble, trouble.

"Hungry?" he asked, his eyes still locked on her.

She blinked, breaking her thoughts, focusing on getting through lunch so she could decide how to proceed later on.

"I can't believe I dragged you this far out of the city," she said mildly, casually checking her menu.

"I was already out here." He was looking at her as though she'd missed a piece of information.

"Oh, right. Why is that?"

"I was hanging out with a friend."

"That's good." Suddenly, she felt a lot less special. Which was silly. She didn't want to feel special. Well, she did. But not in a way that was going to lead to this man breaking her like Steven had with his empty words and unfulfilled promises.

"I'm not sure why I agreed to this," Miranda admitted, avoiding looking at Dak. She'd get locked in, unable to look away, if she did. And then she feared she'd reveal too much. Or agree to more dates.

"You're here because you aren't one to leave a prize unclaimed," he said, his voice low. She peeked around her menu, wishing it was larger and offered more protection from those all-seeing eyes of his. But he lifted his own menu, hiding behind it like her father used to with the business section at the breakfast table. "I like your necklace."

Her fingers found the thin chain, and she tucked it back under the neckline of her sweatshirt where it belonged. It was a simple gold charm less than half the size of her pinkie nail. Her grandmother had worn it every day of her life, one of the few gifts Gramps had been able to afford.

Nobody ever commented on the charm.

"Where'd you get it?" Dak asked.

"I'm not interested in..." Jocks? Small talk? Sharing personal details? Falling in love with a man who'd surely break her heart?

Dak's menu lowered. Their gazes collided, and he gave a smirk, then went back behind his menu.

"What?" she demanded, feeling her cheeks heat.

"Nothing."

She muttered something impolite under her breath and the table shook. It took her a moment to realize it was Dak laughing. She flicked down her menu. His own menu hit the table, and she couldn't help it—the way his face had lit up with amusement and joy, so open and free—she started laughing too.

"What?" she asked again, not knowing why she was laughing, only that it felt good.

His shoulders lifted along with his hands, palms facing up in a helpless shrug.

"Then why are we laughing?"

"Because you're looking at me like I'm going to ask you to marry me."

"Am not!"

He grew serious, plunking his elbows on the table. He leaned forward, and it felt like he was seeing into her soul. "I don't know the game we're playing. And I don't know the rules."

Her body tensed. *Please don't recognize me. Not yet.*

"Whatever it is," he said, leaning back again, "It doesn't matter."

"Oh."

"Because I like you. And you're fun."

She wondered if she could find a way to discreetly fan herself because it was getting very hot in here. She felt like she was on a rollercoaster. Up, down, sideways.

"I like you, too," she squeaked, trying to act unaffected as she toyed with the white napkin tucked around her cutlery.

"But I think we both know we're holding back secrets."

Her neck cricked, she looked up at him so fast.

"We're here to see if it's worth revealing ourselves to each other."

Miranda stared at him for a long beat, barely breathing.

He nodded as though she'd given him an answer—one he liked—then lifted his menu again. "Because I like you, and you like me, and right now, neither of us wants to ruin that with a heavy dose of secrets or reality."

"We don't?"

He peeked around his menu. "You want to pop this bubble?"

She shook her head hard, once. "No, I want to enjoy it."

She added some sass to her tone while straightening her spine. "I want to have some fun."

"Me too, Slays All Day."

Yeah. She knew his type. She *loved* his type. A man who knew what he wanted and wasn't afraid to shout it out and then compete for it, certain the victory would be his.

But would he give her as much power and autonomy as she wanted in a relationship? Not likely.

He was used to running the show. And she'd recently learned that she liked doing that too.

If he was like other men she'd dated, he'd likely keep up the charming routine until she was hooked on him. Then he'd subtly begin to ignore her enough to test her levels of desperation when it came to receiving his attention. Which would be quite high. Then, secure in knowing she was hooked, he'd do his own thing and live his life as he wished while she'd be forced to change her plans and life in order to keep him.

That was no longer her definition of healthy. She'd spent months confused by Steven's sudden indifference, battling feelings of insignificance and as though she was constantly in the wrong. Once she'd figured out what was going on, she'd confronted Steven only to have him humiliate her with a very public breakup. She hadn't dated since.

And now she was considering a man who was being very up front about them both keeping secrets. Would she ever learn how to attract a man capable of having a healthy relationship with her?

"That's so not going to happen," she muttered to herself.

"What isn't?"

"Nothing."

"Tell me."

"Why?"

"Because we're in a bubble together," he said.

"And it's a happy place. This isn't a happy thought."

"All the more reason to tell me."

"You're a pain in the butt, you know that?"

He smiled. "It's one of my best strengths. I was tested and everything. Came out top of the class."

"Fine. You want to know?"

"I do."

"I'm not going to change my life for you. That's number one on the list."

Dak sat back as though she'd slapped him. But his look was more wounded than angry. "You think I'd ask a woman who can't handle a dog and whose friends call her Ms. Slays All Day to change for me? You think I don't know what I'm getting into? That was my peanut shelling record you beat."

"Was not."

"Would I lie about the results of a competition?"

He wouldn't. Everything that came out of Dak's mouth seemed to be the truth.

But secrets were a good way to kill a fledgling relationship —if that's what they were aiming at.

However, telling him who she was could kill it even faster.

"You're going to be the end of me," she admitted, realizing just how much she really did trust and like this man, despite her reservations.

"Don't worry. The feeling's mutual."

His smile was warm and kind, and that weird shyness that seemed to surface around him rose up again. He seemed to see parts of her nobody else did. It should be scary and leave her feeling out of control. But she loved it and wanted to embrace it.

Maybe she already had.

Dak waved off the waitress with the teased yellow hair who looked like she'd worked here since Opening Day decades ago. "The silver lining, I guess, is that I'm looking for someone who's different."

"That doesn't mean this'll work out." Miranda sighed at the sting of disappointment that welled up with her words. Why was she already so invested in this man? Why did she keep saying things that would surely drive him away? She wanted to have fun, date, enjoy life. And here she was with her first real chance in years, and she was practically lighting the man on fire. "And at some point, being with me will probably embarrass you."

Dak watched her with a steady gaze for a long moment. "I doubt that."

"Well, life is full of surprises."

He chuckled. "That it is. And you might soon discover that my life's direction and purpose is up for debate." He shook his head as though frustrated with himself. "Sorry, it's a first date. You don't want to hear about the deep mess I call my brain."

"That's okay. The happy bubble, right?"

"The bubble," he confirmed.

"So what are we doing? Just having fun until it's time to pop the bubble?"

He smiled. "I'm game if you are."

He closed his menu and leaned forward, his grin so full of life that she couldn't help but stop fighting her doubts and let go.

MIRANDA WAS LAUGHING, her BLT forgotten, her face lighting up in a way Dak had never seen on TV. It could get addicting making this woman laugh.

So far she'd called him on what they were doing: hiding their secrets and pretending a relationship might work out by doing so.

Had Dak spent so much of his life in the sheltered shadow of the NHL that this woman, who had single-handedly upset so many in the league with her mere presence, seemed normal? He liked to believe he still had a handle on how real life worked, but she definitely wasn't the woman he'd assumed she was. She could buy any place in the city, from what he could tell, and she was hanging out in Sweetheart Creek.

He was flattered by how, despite hiding her identity from him, she was letting him into her private life. He knew what a privilege that was. But what he'd done to earn it, he had no idea. He just hoped he didn't mess it up.

The craziest thing was that since meeting Miranda, he could no longer ignore his doubts about the café being a suitable replacement dream for playing in the NHL. Sure, the café would never be as exciting as high-level hockey, but it was nice sleeping in his own bed every night rather than in a hotel after a late game before hopping a flight home so he could turn around and do it all again. He liked that part. But he felt unfulfilled.

And maybe that's what his pal Maverick saw that had caused him to set Dak up with the job interview with Miranda's charity.

Maybe hockey truly was a vital piece of him, and walking away was denying a large part of who he was. The game had been his home and mistress his entire adult life with the exception of the past year. It had always been his identity, his sense of self as well as his social life. Maybe Mav was onto something and Dak wasn't supposed to completely avoid the NHL as a way of finding himself.

He was on a date with a team owner and loving it, after all.

Although dating Miranda wouldn't be easy. He'd have to flex and bend for her, and her life, more than he was used to.

He gave himself a shake. What was he thinking? This was a first date, and he hadn't even interviewed for the player-hospital liaison position for her charity yet. He was moving too darn fast again. Just like he had with Jari. Their marriage happened quickly. He'd been so certain about the future he saw, thinking the two of them were truly on the same page. Turned out 'dealing with real life and fame' meant something very different to Jari.

Right now Dak needed to chill out before he did something crazy like propose marriage to Miranda because of the connection he felt with her.

He focused back on Miranda, whose attention was caught on the diner's TV. It looked as though they were streaming Texas college football. He'd heard a few people mention a kid named Hernandez, who he gathered must be local.

"I bet he makes the pass," Miranda said.

Dak watched the player's body language for a moment. "Bet he doesn't."

"Just to be a contrarian?" she asked without looking away from the game.

"He's psyching himself out. He's got too much riding on this."

The man at the next table frowned at Dak before focusing back on the screen.

Miranda watched the ongoing play, eyes narrowing. Dak could see the moment she spotted what he was talking about and her jaw went slack with empathy and concern. Dak wished the ball into the receiver's outstretched hands as he sprinted toward it.

Missed pass.

The man at the table beside them swore.

"He needs a mindset coach," Miranda said with a sigh.

Dak hadn't expected her to care about some kid's success on a team she probably didn't even follow. It made him curious about the rumors about how player-centric she was with her own team. Maverick said she cared about her guys from their home life to ice life. She'd brought in life coaches, sports psychologists, financial advisors, and accountants to assist them.

Would Dak's own rookie years have been different if he'd been on a team like hers instead of given a few million at nineteen and told to go live it up?

"How do you know so much about sports?" Dak asked.

"My grandpa used to take me to games."

"Football?"

"Yeah. And baseball, boxing, wrestling…"

"Really?"

She nodded. She wouldn't look away from the screen, and he wondered what she was hiding. He'd already learned she wouldn't make eye contact when she was scared or afraid to reveal something.

Happy bubble.

"Is he the one who made you the competitive fiend you are today?"

She grinned and looked his way. "He helped nurture that side of me, yes. Much to my mother's chagrin." She lifted the colored plastic cup that had been filled with water. "Did you know I'm a stacking contest champ with these?"

He glanced at the cup, pretty sure she was trying to divert

him from what was likely a deeper, more sensitive subject. Or from revealing who she really was.

"Yeah?" he asked, playing along.

"This other camp counselor, Melanie Summer, and I didn't feel like swimming during one of our camp counselor training breaks so we made up this whole game."

"Melanie Summer?"

"Yeah. At Camp Adaker? Ever heard of it?" She was teasing him, but the coincidence that they both knew Melanie as well as the camp felt weird.

"Actually, I have. Melanie resurrected the camp a few years ago. It was about to close."

"What?"

"Yeah, she got all these—" Dak froze. He'd done some promo for the camp during his years playing for Toronto. But Miranda didn't know he was NHL, and he wasn't ready to burst their happy bubble yet.

"These what?"

"Well, people to help her get things going again."

"How do you know all of this?" Miranda demanded.

He frowned good-naturedly. "I'm Canadian. Remember? We all know each other."

She snorted and rolled her eyes but let it go. "Anyway, we could stack these cups higher than our heads before they fell over."

"Tell me about your mother's chagrin and your secret competitive persona. It sounds like a titillating superhero origin story."

She sighed softly. "Nothing that grand. She just said it's not very ladylike to always be challenging people."

"And so did you stop?"

"What do you think?" She grinned.

"Well, based on my short experience of knowing you, I'd say Mom lost that battle."

Miranda laughed, and the earlier stress that had edged into her expression melted.

They stared at each other for a long moment.

"You surprise me," she said.

"Feeling's mutual."

"I want to ask you a lot of things right now."

"But the bubble?" he joked, knowing that the moment they shared who they really were, everything would change. Everything.

"I don't want this to end."

"Neither do I." He reached across the table, tangling his fingers in hers.

He wanted to learn everything about this woman.

"DID you ever get suspended from school?" Dak asked as he waited for the waitress to come back with his credit card.

Miranda had challenged him to a game of Paper, Rock, Scissors—winner paid for lunch. He'd gotten a sexy, determined look in his eyes, played, lost, insisted they play best out of three, lost again, and then refused to let her pay.

He was adorable.

"Do I look like the type to get in trouble?" she asked.

"The type to ignore a dare? Not a chance. And I bet at least one went south on you, and I bet you've been asked to stay home for a few days. At least once."

She stared at him for a long moment, fighting the way the corner of her lips wanted to turn up. This man seemed to know her a little too well in all the right ways. It made her want to kiss him to see if he knew what she'd like in that department. She had a feeling he would.

"Twice." She leaned against the table, shielding her face with a hand, embarrassed.

"Did Daddy take away your car?"

She dropped her hand. "I *don't* call him Daddy. And anyway, I hated that car." She shuddered dramatically, and he laughed. "He only took it away until I spilled tears and convinced him it wasn't my fault."

"He bought that?"

"It was a long walk to school; I was motivated." She leaned forward. "And how many times did *you* get kicked out?"

"Never, actually. I missed too much being on the—"

"The what?"

He shrugged and laughed.

"Tractor?"

He shook his head, still laughing. "Secrets, remember?"

"You were in juvie?" she teased, knowing it wasn't true but curious if he'd reveal some personal history despite their self-imposed bubble.

"Never." He was so serious, Miranda wished she hadn't joked. The waitress appeared with Dak's card, and Miranda gathered her purse and edged forward in her seat.

"Am I allowed to know where to find you?" Dak asked, not standing. "You know where I work."

"Nope." No way. "But I live just outside of town. Everyone here knows where I live. I'm sure they'd give me up in a heartbeat."

"It would be a lot of work dating you," Dak said, leaning back and tossing his paper napkin on the table.

"Is this not a date?"

"Is there a kiss at the end?"

"I don't know. Is there?"

"Ms. Slays All Day and Doesn't Change for Anyone doesn't instigate kisses at the end of her dates?"

"She does if she wants one."

"Well, I dare you to kiss me later."

"How much later?"

"How much later do you want?" he asked.

"Ready to go?"

"Eager to kiss me?" Dak grinned as he escorted her out, his warm hand on her lower back. It felt just as delicious as she'd expected it to. "I can get behind that, even though it means our date will be over sooner."

On the sidewalk in front of the diner, they faltered, neither of them wanting the date to end.

"Look at that," Dak said, frowning into the distance. An armadillo waddled its way across the road, challenging a pickup truck, which waited patiently for it to move off the street.

"That's Bill. He's a bit of a character, I hear. There's even a drink named after him at the saloon." Miranda pointed to a building on the other side of the road and down a way. It was weathered and looked like it might have been the town's first original business.

"Really?"

She nodded, and they shifted awkwardly.

"I usually kill it on dates," Dak murmured.

"You go on a lot?"

"Not an unhealthy amount."

"What's a healthy amount? Ballpark figure?"

"You're gorgeous. Confident. I like that you're not about to fall at my feet and worship me."

"Really? So compliments to duck answering that question?

Must be a *lot* of dates." She put a hand on a hip and studied him. "You were very good at dropping tantalizing talents the other day, such as cooking, including cooking at a homeless shelter. I bet that's tasty date bait for a man looking to get kissed."

He chuckled and had the grace to look embarrassed. "I don't date a ton. And for the record, you *are* gorgeous. I didn't mean to use my volunteerism as bait." He leaned closer. "But…did it work? Or at least help?"

She let out a soft laugh. "It earned you a point. Or two. I like it when people help others."

"Me too." He took her hand, entwining their fingers like he had at the table. It felt natural to be connected.

"And FYI, even though I'm sure you already know this and have heard it a ton, you're kinda hot, too."

"Kinda?" He acted wounded, swooning like he'd been physically struck, using the move to draw her closer. "Most women drool when they see me."

"Okay, a lot hot. But don't let it go to your head. And FYI, I never drool."

"Noted."

"Thank you."

They grew quiet, as though deciding whether to kiss. That was the trouble with a lunch date. It never felt like a date-date. It had too much of a business vibe or a just-friends vibe.

Miranda ran her fingers down the cotton placket of his shirt, toying with the buttons, edging ever so slightly closer, making it easier for a kiss to happen.

"I saw you eyeing my shirt," Dak said without looking down. "You think I'm high maintenance, don't you?"

"I wondered about possible money laundering habits." She leaned into him, looking up.

He let out a loud guffaw of laughter. "Nice."

"It's true." She shook her head, letting on that she hadn't actually thought that.

"I like you." He smiled down at her. Amidst their joking, they'd moved so close they were almost in an embrace.

"You do?" He smelled great. Like the gingerbread cookies from his café, like lattes and vanilla sweetener. All items that could be found on her favorite things list.

"You know who you are," he murmured. "I admire that."

"I'm also high maintenance. And busy."

"So am I."

She leaned in, supporting herself against him.

"I keep trying to find ways to prove that you're not the kind of woman I'm looking for. But you keep leaving me like a dazzled baboon."

She laughed lightly, tickled that she might have that kind of power over a man like him.

"Then why don't you burst the bubble and carry on with life?" she murmured, looking up at him, hoping he'd reject her suggestion and kiss her instead.

"I keep trying to convince myself to do that."

"So why don't you?"

"I don't know."

Her hand was still entwined in his, and he used it to pull her tight to him. His head tipped down, his lips meeting hers. She resisted for a split second, afraid of how good this moment might feel and how much it might throw her off her vow to let this end before it got messy.

But when his arms swept around her, she was lost in the warmth of him. In his arms, she felt safe. That connection that had been buzzing between them surged, strengthened, and blasted through her like an unstoppable current. Miranda gasped, and the kiss deepened. She lost all awareness of where she was, only that she was with Dak and she never wanted to be without him.

They broke the kiss, Dak looking as off balance as she felt. Dazed and a little bit blown away.

"I know why I haven't burst the bubble and gone home," he said.

"Why's that?"

"Because when I'm with you, I know what I want in my life. And one of those things I want is this difficult, funny, sweet, and powerful woman who challenges me at every single turn, even if she makes me crazy."

"Well, I'll let you know if I find her."

He smiled down at her. "I already did. She's in my arms."

Miranda finally let loose the smile she'd been fighting. She didn't mind Dak knowing that she loved kissing him, loved his sweet words, and loved that he'd basically just poured the equivalent of catnip in her lap while referring to her empowerment. He might actually be the one for her.

Her smile grew bigger.

He gently stroked her cheek, his body warm against hers. "And every time you smile like that, I feel as if I've won something nobody else has. I want to stay in this bubble with you for a very long time."

CHAPTER 3

Miranda rolled her shoulders, trying to relax on Monday morning as she waited for the elevator to take her to her top-floor office at the Dragons' headquarters. The chair of her new charity's board had called in sick, so on top of her usual Monday morning catch-up, she was stepping in to run this morning's interview for the player-hospital liaison position.

"Who was the weekend hottie?" Daisy-Mae asked, joining Miranda at the elevators.

"He was yummy," Violet said, hitting the Up button again even though it was already lit up. Her smooth, shoulder-length black hair cascaded around her face as she moved, and Miranda found herself wishing her hair would curtain with perfection like Violet's. Instead, hers tended toward a wonky wave unless threatened with products and hot irons.

"His name's Dak." The elevator doors opened, and she entered. "Do y'all know him? I can't shake the feeling I've met him somewhere. But I know I haven't." She smiled as she thought of Saturday's goodbye kiss with Dak. Along with the promise of a Wednesday lunch date, she had been buoyed all of yesterday. She was falling for this guy whether she wanted to or not.

"Maybe you met at an event?" Violet offered, her dark eyes full of curiosity.

"You'd remember him," Daisy-Mae said with a waggle of her eyebrows as they settled into the elevator. "That man's…*everything*…is unforgettable!"

"I was thinking I'd do a little online stalking after I finish this interview for the charity." Although not knowing Dak's last name could make her stalking trickier. Then again, she was certain she'd easily find him if he truly owned Gingerbread Café.

Miranda selected the buttons for the top floor, then the fourth floor for Violet and Daisy-Mae.

"You haven't checked him out yet?" Violet asked, aghast. She hit the floor buttons Miranda had already selected.

"No, why?" Miranda asked.

"You have to. Men are so…" She shuddered.

"Bad experience?"

"The worst," Daisy-Mae supplied as Violet went silent, her expression dark. Violet jabbed the Close Door button three times, before crossing her arms in front of her. From the side of her mouth, Daisy-Mae muttered, "It'll be a miracle if Violet dates again."

"I'll get there," Violet grit out as the elevator doors closed. "I flirt, don't I?"

"Yeah, but if anyone ever asked you out, you'd faint."

Violet rolled her gorgeous deep brown eyes so hard and with such aggression, Miranda nearly laughed. Violet could be shy, but more often she was charming and bubbly—except for today. She seemed ready to tiger-pounce someone. And yet, Miranda could still imagine her fainting if one of her big, burly players asked her out.

"I'm sorry," Miranda said, unsure what else to say.

"Yeah, well," Daisy-Mae said easily as the elevator jerked upward, then downward an inch or two, apparently undecided about delivering them to their chosen floors. "Oomph. What's with the elevator?"

Violet stabbed various buttons, trying to get it to move.

"All I know is that there's no point pining over a man," she said, "because if you do, when he runs back to baseball he'll never even know you were crushing on him! What a waste!"

"So you're going to check out the hottie?" Daisy-Mae asked Miranda, swiftly changing the topic.

The doors jerked open a few inches, then hesitated. Before Violet could attack the panel of buttons again, large hands reached between the gap, pulling the doors the rest of the way open.

"Oh, sorry," Violet said, as Maverick Blades walked in wearing a suit jacket and jeans. His gaze lingered on Daisy-Mae, and she breathed a hello. He nodded and said good morning to the women before facing the already closing doors, hands clasped in front of him.

"Top floor, please," he said to Violet. She pointed to the lit-up button, then gave it an extra double poke for good measure.

"Where did you meet him?" Daisy-Mae asked Miranda.

"At that sports pub-café place down on Ryerson."

"Gingerbread Café?" Daisy-Mae asked, clearly delighted. "You went?"

"I did."

"Great Caesars," Daisy-Mae stated.

"I like the cookies," Violet added.

Maverick twisted his torso slightly, looking at them over his shoulder.

"I read an article about the owner," Violet said in a thoughtful tone. "Dakarais...something?" The doors opened on the fourth floor, and she impatiently hit the Close Door button until the elevator complied and continued its ascent.

"Dakarai Morisette," Maverick said, still looking straight ahead.

"You know him?" Miranda asked, her stomach sinking. What if he was an NHL player? She had strict rules about dating players.

No. No, he wasn't a player. He ran a café. He didn't have time to play in the NHL. She was just looking for reasons not to fall for Dak.

The elevator doors opened on the top floor and, to Miranda's surprise, everyone exited.

"Dak and I go way back," Maverick said, his gaze tracking Daisy-Mae, making the woman blush. "We were on a farm team together before we were called up."

"Called up to where? What's a farm team?" Violet whispered to Daisy-Mae.

"He retired almost a year ago. Forced out. Injury," Maverick said to Miranda.

"It's where the teams get their players," Daisy-Mae whispered back to Violet.

"Retired from..." Miranda asked, dreading his answer. She knew what a farm team was. Knew what being called up meant. Dak was verified NHL.

"Meeting in three," Miranda's assistant called to her, making a point of checking his watch. He then waved a stack of notes. Messages. That was the one thing about hiding out all weekend. Monday mornings became a marathon.

She nodded, turning back to the women to finish their conversation.

The man she was falling for was NHL. Didn't that figure? But he was retired. Did that make a difference?

Oh no. She froze.

He knew who she was.

And hadn't said a thing.

She glanced around the empty waiting area. Nobody present but people she'd already hired. No interview candidate. She had time before the interview to drill Maverick about Dak.

She squared herself to him as Maverick said, "He was Toronto's main D-man for years."

"Defenseman," she said.

"The best."

She'd ignored her gut feelings about Dak being a pro athlete, adoring the way he seemed to understand her and her joy of competition.

Did it matter that he'd once played? Wasn't that a good thing? Wasn't that part of what helped them click?

By playing along with their happy bubble game, did that make him respectful or deceitful?

"Thank you," Miranda said to Maverick.

He nodded, giving Daisy-Mae one of those lingering gazes again before checking in with Miranda's receptionist. Right. Maverick was bringing in a friend for the interview and had agreed to sit in to answer any questions related to the players' involvement in the charity.

"You *have* to cyberstalk him now," Violet muttered. "Think of all the women players have falling all over them."

Miranda really didn't want to think about that.

Daisy-Mae hit the button to summon the elevator to take them down to the fourth floor. "We have a meeting, Vi."

"Hey, why don't you date Maverick?" Violet whispered, turning to Daisy-Mae. "He has elevator magic. Did you see how fast it moved once he was in it?" She wiggled her fingers as though they possessed magical powers. "*And* he was giving you extra long looks."

"He was just confused by my makeover." She gestured to her business attire. "He's never seen me dressing the part of city businesswoman."

"You should ask him out," Miranda said. Her publicity team wanted to give Maverick a makeover of his own. And last she'd heard, they wanted to marry him off which was pretty extreme in her opinion. Maybe a few dates with someone sweet like Daisy-Mae would do the trick.

"No," Daisy-Mae said with a shake of her head. Violet gave her a pleading look and Daisy-Mae began listing things off on her fingers. "He's out of my league, I'm not his type, and he's best friends with my ex—a guy I dated for years. That would just be awkward."

Violet sighed. "You think too much." She returned her attention to Miranda. "How Dak interacts with women on social media will tell you everything you need to know about him."

Miranda already knew how he interacted with women in real life—her. And he'd been perfect.

Except he surely knew who she was, which meant she'd never fooled him with the I'm-just-some-normal-gal routine, had she?

But he'd fooled her with his I'm-just-some-normal-guy routine.

"How can his café be less than a year old?" Miranda asked,

huddling with the women. "It's littered with awards." She paused and rolled her eyes. "Of course it is. He's super competitive. Like me." She crossed her arms. Two peas in a pod. Another reason it would never work out. It got too crowded.

He was a man who wanted the bling and the public acknowledgment that he was the best at whatever he was doing.

She didn't fault him for that. She wanted the Stanley Cup, after all.

But what about her? Was she just a trophy to a man like Dak? An elite-level buckle bunny conquest? She knew her professional position could give men bragging rights and status. But Dak…

That didn't fit what she knew of him.

But why hadn't he said something about who she was? Why wouldn't he tell her he was retired NHL?

She was so done with men hiding who they really were.

She winced as she realized she wasn't any better.

She had a solid reason though. She didn't want him changing and acting all charming because she had money. Money was wonderful, but it got in the way of a good first date.

And yet, he'd known exactly who she was and what she had. Thinking back, he'd even baited her in conversation a time or two. Asked why she knew sports. Called her a dragon slayer.

And she hadn't fessed up. She was a hypocrite if she was going to be upset with Dak and his own NHL secrets.

"When's your next date?" Daisy-Mae asked.

Miranda crossed her arms. "Never."

"What?" Violet looked startled. "Why?"

"I don't date players."

"Mav says he retired," Daisy-Mae pointed out.

"Doesn't matter."

She'd let herself be blinded. She'd ignored her instincts and thought their bubble of secrets was only protecting her.

Of course he was a hockey player. They were as tough as nails, skating through all kinds of pain to put out their best for their fans and the team. Players had incredible hearts, and she'd seen that in Dak. Recognized it. Ignored it.

And now here she was, falling for a man she didn't actually know.

"You've already dated him," Violet pointed out.

"And liked him." Daisy-Mae added.

"Doesn't matter. A rule is a rule."

"Rule obliterated." Daisy-Mae laughed and Miranda scowled.

"No. A rule is a rule." Especially for men who hid their identities and let her play the fool.

DAK WAITED FOR THE ELEVATOR, frustrated that he was running late for his job interview after first waffling on whether or not to come and then having the location changed on him last minute. He eyed the door to the stairs. Not that many flights. Which would be faster?

"I'm here now." A woman, done up to the hilt, joined him at the elevators and impatiently hit the Up button even though it was already glowing. "I said I'd take her out to lunch to figure out what's going on, and I *will*, Mom." There was silence as she listened to someone on the other end of the line. "Maybe she's making a point for that comment Dad made on her birthday. Just because she bought a house with only two bedrooms—" The woman sighed and said tiredly, "She's fine. She's different—not cracking psychologically." She rolled her eyes toward Dak and he politely smiled, trying his best to ignore her end of the conversation.

The elevator doors opened, and Dak allowed the woman to enter first.

Inside, she jabbed the button for the top floor and glanced at Dak, who nodded.

There was silence, a sigh, another eye roll. "It's not attention seeking, Mom." She stared at the ceiling of the elevator as though trying to hold her patience.

Dak tried to hide his amusement.

"Well, at least I'm married. It's got to be awful for Lorelei being single. The comments everyone's making around the country club have to be hard to take. At least Miranda *wants* to be single."

Miranda? *His* Miranda? Dak's vow to stop eavesdropping ended. He knew Miranda was currently in this building somewhere. She might even be laughing at the email he'd sent her earlier that morning. And this woman beside him was going to go see her. On the top floor. Where his meeting was.

His heart thrummed faster. Was his interview with Miranda now? Had she figured out he was the applicant and so was interviewing him herself?

"She didn't say *that*." The woman laughed with a similar warmth to Miranda, removing any doubt that she was related. "Mir just has unrealistic expectations of relationships. She wants a guy who *gets* her. She'll give up eventually."

He hoped not. Everyone should find someone who understood them. He personally wanted that as well as someone who would push and challenge him to be all that he could be. There'd never be anything wrong with that.

The doors opened on the top floor, and Dak followed the woman into the open lobby. Windows faced him from behind a receptionist's desk, and offices lined the walls to his left and right.

The woman from the elevator marched straight into an office on the left while an assistant sputtered and chased after her, reaching her in time to have the door closed in his face.

If this was Miranda's family life, then Dak was starting to understand why she was escaping to Sweetheart Creek whenever she could.

He straightened his blazer, giving the cuffs a tug. Miranda was becoming a problem. The more he learned about her, the more he felt she was a black sheep with a good heart who needed someone in her corner. Someone like him.

The problem was that he'd promised himself he was done with the high-pressure, fast-paced world of the NHL. He was ready for real life with a wife, kids, and a family calendar outlined in various colors. But he meant what he'd said to Miranda on the weekend. He wanted a woman who held her own, even if he sometimes had to slow down and let her into the fast lane ahead of him.

Dak spied Maverick sitting on the low, black leather couches set to the side near the windows. The office to Dak's right was the player development and scouting coordinator, and he longed to peek his head inside.

Instead, he joined Maverick.

"Was starting to think you were standing me up." Maverick stood, shaking his hand while giving him a slap on the shoulder.

"Considered it," Dak admitted.

"Hope the last-minute change in location didn't throw you."

"Any word why?" Dak eyed the door where the woman from the elevator had disappeared. He was fairly confident that soon he'd be facing a brutal personal moment of truth. Miranda would be within her rights if she was angry at him for not letting on that a) he knew her, b) he was former NHL, and c) he was interviewing to work in her charity.

She'd be within her rights to kick him out. After yelling at him first.

But at least he could go back to his café and be happy. Right?

Except he really wanted to work with Miranda. He wanted to be a part of whatever it was she was building here. He wanted to be a part of the NHL again. Even the posters, jerseys, and signed sticks on the lobby walls felt familiar and like home. This was where he belonged, where he spoke the language and understood the nuances and how to navigate.

Being with Miranda for those few short hours had given him this clarity.

"Your name was mentioned in the elevator on my way up," Maverick said. "By Miranda. Miranda Fairchild."

Dak's focus moved from how nervous he was to his friend's words. "Sorry? What?"

"She didn't know who you are," Maverick said, watching him steadily.

Then why had his interview been moved here?

"I really hope you don't think I'll serve as your human shield during this meeting," Maverick stated.

He was meeting with Miranda. Oh, wow.

"I'll explain," Dak promised.

"Yeah? Right before she kicks you to the moon? Or are you going to tell her on your way back down again? She's wearing some pretty lethal looking heels today."

"Okay, so I got caught up in things." Dak pushed himself back into the couch. "I wasn't thinking."

"Obviously." Maverick gave him a look best described as disappointed. "You knew who she was. And you dated her. Why would you keep her in the dark about who you are?"

He ran a hand down his face. "I didn't mean to."

He'd totally gotten caught up in Miranda and their games, not even considering how real the consequences might be. Their little bubble had seemed cute and harmless in Sweetheart Creek, but here and now, it was just another reason they shouldn't date. That and the impending hate-on coming his way.

"I can walk away." He considered the statement, nodding. He could still do that.

His friend whooped with laughter. "You can walk away?" Maverick scanned around the waiting area as though looking for backup. The receptionist, on the phone, shot him a glare and spun his chair, putting his back to them.

The way Maverick was laughing was riling his anger.

"What?" he snapped.

"I'll bet the two of you are always trying to one-up each other. And that she's the reason you've been smiling lately. I'll bet—"

"Okay, enough." Dak pushed against the couch back, sliding his hands down his thighs. "Yeah, she's competitive. And she brings it out in me, too. I don't like it."

"I don't like it," Maverick mocked, using the same pouty tone Dak had. "Because you don't enjoy losing to a woman?" Dak's expression must have betrayed how much Dak liked her because Maverick eased up. "Come on, she's the first worthy opponent you've had since Jari. Miranda makes you laugh and do something other than moan about how the café is your dream, so why aren't you happy?"

"I don't moan about that! It *is* my dream and I am happy." Even he could hear the lack of conviction in his voice.

"You're obviously lost and unhappy. Is it possible you jumped in too fast? And that your own café wasn't really what you wanted or needed?"

"What else was I supposed to do? My career ended."

Maverick was silent for a long beat. "You've been like my old buddy again this week."

"I know," Dak said glumly. It was true. He'd been full of energy and smiles since meeting Miranda. She mattered to him—a lot more than she should after only seeing her twice.

And their upcoming encounter was also going to matter a whole lot, too. Sadly, he didn't believe he deserved much in the forgiveness department.

Which meant he was soon to lose Miranda.

And he'd be back to the café again.

"I'm still your buddy," Dak said, jiggling his knee and rolling his right shoulder, "but I don't need to get all caught up in competition with some woman to be that guy." He lowered his voice, gesturing to Miranda's closed door. "She might become my boss. And besides, what kind of man competes with their girlfriend all the time?"

"You really think she's going to keep a deceitful liar? A man who can't even take a shot on an empty net?"

"I'd just crushed my shoulder! I couldn't move my right arm!"

"You're so easy." Maverick grinned so wide Dak could practically see his molars. Dak clasped his right fist in his left hand. He really wanted to send his friend to the dentist for riling him up like that.

Maverick sobered, looking both directions before leaning over the small table that separated the two couches. "She's your girlfriend?"

He stared hard at Maverick, then shook his head. "I think I lost that chance."

"WHAT'S UP, DEANNA?" Miranda asked as her office door opened and closed. Her sister had just blown past her assistant again. So much for having someone guard her door against intrusions. Then again, her sister tended to be an unstoppable force.

"We're going for lunch," her sister announced, presenting herself in front of Miranda with a flourish.

"It's only nine, and I have a meeting."

"With those hunks in your waiting area?"

"Probably." There were a lot of fit, hunky men in her line of business.

"I'll tell them something came up and to rebook." Deanna moved to open the door, but Miranda gave her a sharp no.

She received a wounded look.

"Mom's worried about you." Deanna threw herself into the armchair across from Miranda, kicking her legs over the chair's arm like she was a teenager and not twenty-eight, married, and supposedly too proper to slouch or sit like that in a skirt.

Obviously, Deanna was her favorite sister.

"Daddy thinks this whole thing"—she gestured to the office and the company at large—"and that charity you started is about tax write-offs and bankruptcy."

Miranda sighed and gave her sister a look which resulted in a smirk.

"You really want to smash the patriarchy, don't you?" Deanna asked, a slightly evil glint flashing in her eyes.

Miranda laughed. "I outgrew that phase a long time ago."

Her sister gestured to Miranda's plum-colored walls and the floral print chairs in front of her desk and smirked. "I doubt that. Your décor is totally snubbing its nose at the testosterone levels around here." She stood up. "Oh, and wait… How many female team owners are there in the NHL again?" She feigned thoughtfulness, her thumb and pointer finger cradling her chin.

Miranda laughed again. "I want to hang out with you, but I can't just blow off these meetings."

She pouted. "You know I can't make Mom think you're fine forever if you don't come out for lunch with me."

"I *am* fine. Really. And we'll have lunch…" She quickly ran through her mental schedule. "Friday? No, Wednesday." She was canceling her lunch date with Dak. Because seriously.

"Are you dating?"

Miranda felt her face flush. "When did that become an indicator of whether I'm okay?"

"After Steven."

"What?"

"We're worried about you. Since he broke up with you in front of everyone at that fundraiser—"

"Gala." She still hated galas for that reason. Among a few other reasons. And yet, here she was, organizing one for next month because she knew it would boost her charity.

"Sure, whatever it was. You've been doing weird things ever since then."

"Have not."

"Tiny house, dirt driveway—"

"Not weird."

"The struggling new NHL team. This is a sport you've never even played. A sport most people here have never played because we're in Texas! It's hot. It's sticky. It's dry. No snow. No ice. That's weird."

Okay, she'd give her that one.

"And you never come to the country club anymore. You won't come to fundraisers if Steven and his fiancée are going to be there. And you haven't brought a man home since Steven, which was almost two years ago."

"I've been busy. I'm not avoiding him and Sugar Lips."

She kind of was.

"I know he hurt you when he didn't stand up for you at that fundraiser—"

"I really don't want to talk about it."

"—and when he called your ideas silly for wanting to start a team."

"Deanna…"

"He's a jerk for dumping you because he couldn't handle his friends' reactions. It just shows that he wasn't the right man for you."

"Thanks."

"So what's really going on? Some sort of life crisis? A big, long pout until Daddy approves of you owning a team?"

Miranda sighed. "I'm just tired of trying to fit in and doing the quiet, pretty, agreeable thing."

"Did you actually try?" Deanna said with a snort. She caught Miranda's dark glare.

"I just want to live my life like I'm *doing* something with it. Like I'm being *me*. I swear I'm not crazy."

Deanna stood, hitching her designer bag higher on her shoulder. "If you want to get back at Daddy—"

"I don't."

"Then just find a nice man at the club."

Miranda sighed.

Her sister held up a finger like she expected Miranda to argue. "One who doesn't get embarrassed by your plethora of opinions and ideas like Steven did."

Miranda nodded. "They're hard to find."

Deanna paused at the door. "I just don't get it."

"Get what?"

"You want to create a legacy for Gramps. But how is running a team of rich men who slam into each other really going to do that? Is it really leaving the world a better place like you keep saying it will?"

"I want to help players be prepared in case their careers suddenly go south."

"Boo-hoo for these *white* men living the American dream. Go patriarchy and male dominance and privilege and all those things you used to rant about when you were sixteen. Go make your difference, Mir. Change the world. Go you."

"I started a charity for sick kids!" she called loudly as Deanna closed the door behind her.

Her sister opened the door again, saying, "Easy target! Easy win!"

"Winning isn't everything!" Miranda snapped to the closed door.

She propped her elbows on the desk, holding her head. How was it after one brief conversation with Deanna, her whole entire *everything* felt futile and without purpose?

CHAPTER 4

Dak straightened his shoulders, wished himself luck, and followed Maverick through the office door being held open by Miranda's assistant. Dak gave the man a nod, bracing himself as he faced Miranda as well as his own betrayal.

Secrets. They were never a good thing.

He'd done everything wrong with the first woman to intrigue him in a very long time—maybe truly ever.

Miranda stood from behind a massive desk and came around to the front of it. She extended her hand, giving Maverick's a shake, then Dak's.

She held Dak's hand a little longer than Maverick's and held his gaze, too. "You knew who I was."

It was a statement, devoid of emotion, blame, hurt, or any of the things he would've expected. It was like a shield had gone up and she was assessing him the way she would a spreadsheet. This was Ms. Slays All Day, not the sweet Miranda he had quickly come to know.

There was also no yelling. No kicking him out. No well-deserved rant.

It gave him a ridiculous amount of hope.

He swallowed, realizing this could actually be a trap, specially laid for him to walk into and seal up on his own.

"I suspected when you first came into the Gingerbread Café," Dak confessed, grateful his brain had opted for honesty, not some lame attempt at a cover-up.

"And you didn't say something. Why?" She looked like the woman he saw on TV. Composed. Her wardrobe and makeup worn as armor.

Maverick shifted, edging toward the closed door. "I'll just pop out, shall I?"

Miranda turned to him, her gaze steely. "Stay." Her dark eyes returned to Dak.

He chose his next words carefully. This was an important moment. Not for the job he was here to interview for, but for their fledgling relationship.

"We both acknowledged we have secrets," he said. She crossed her arms, and he realized he was shifting the blame, making excuses. But it was also the truth. "We were in our happy bubble. We danced around who we really are because we didn't want real life to intrude on the connection we were building.

"I admit I did everything wrong. I know that. I didn't expect to feel a connection with you. And I didn't realize I'd want to explore it beyond the walls of my café, and even beyond the walls of the diner. I would do things differently if I had a do-over. I'm sorry I wasn't up front, Miranda."

Her lips pressed together as though holding back emotion. She said nothing in return, and if this hadn't been a business meeting, if his best friend hadn't been standing at his elbow, he would have reached for her.

"You didn't tell me who you were." Her voice was firm but had an unsteady vibration to it.

"Actually, I was hoping to leave this part of my life behind." He gestured to the purple wall to his left, where NHL paraphernalia hung along with the recent team photo. "I didn't leave this world the way I'd always envisioned."

To his surprise, her expression turned sympathetic and full of understanding.

"This was the only life I knew for a very long time. I'm trying to move on and experience what they call real life." He scrubbed a hand through his hair. "I promise I wasn't trying to deceive you. It may sound lame, but I was trying to protect myself as well as honor your need for secrets."

Maverick was watching them, his head lowered, peering through his brows as though attempting to make himself invisible while also not wanting to miss a thing.

Dak forced his shoulders straight, meeting Miranda's eye as she continued to stare at him.

"You realize this position doesn't offer you a way back into the life?" she said. "Not in the jersey-wearing sense."

He nodded. She was politely calling him on his lame excuse—even though his reasoning felt valid.

"Maverick has said great things about you, but if you're not interested in returning to a team in any capacity, then I understand, and I apologize for wasting your time."

She was kicking him out.

It made him adore her all the more.

She moved to stand behind her desk, her lavender and black dress clinging to her every plush curve. And even though he preferred the lower maintenance version of

Miranda, he had to say Ms. Slays All Day was the sexiest thing he'd seen in eons.

Maverick cleared his throat. "Dak has been through a lot as a player. He understands how the sudden rise and shift in lifestyle can really throw a rookie." Despite the praise, his heart didn't seem to be in it. He was probably wondering if vouching for Dak would impact his career. "He knows how important it is to have something meaningful in your life. Something solid and real that gives you perspective. Having somewhere that you're contributing selflessly can ground you, sober you. And working with sick kids is all of the above. Dak has also worked with various charities over the years."

"So I've heard," Miranda said.

"He has the right understanding and knowledge," Maverick continued, "to work as the go-between for your players, the hospital, and their patients."

Miranda sat, her killer heels hidden and out of striking distance. Seeing that she was listening to Maverick, and seemed less intent on dismissing the men, Dak eased into one of the flower-print chairs across from her desk, wishing she would meet his gaze.

"Not everyone on the team is excited about giving up their free time to work with kids, let alone kids who are sick," Miranda said. "It's uncomfortable and difficult."

"I know," Dak said. "And you can't force your players to participate. But I believe there's a way we can all help, whether it's in the childrens' ward or behind the scenes. I also believe that helping is good for the players. I know charity work would have benefited me during my rookie years."

"How so?"

Dak took a moment to consider his words, feeling Miranda's gaze press into him. "My cousin and I were deep into the party lifestyle, enjoying all life had thrown at us. He was in the NFL and I was in the NHL. We felt like we'd hit the jackpot."

"And?"

"He died in a car crash, and I married a woman who didn't truly love me."

"You're married?"

"Divorced," he and Maverick said at the same time.

Dak locked eyes with Miranda. "My cousin's death woke me up, and I was able to turn my life around, save my career and a bit of money. I was also able to share some of the good that had come my way."

Miranda said nothing, and he wondered if she'd researched him before the meeting. If she already knew his deep, dark secrets. Somehow, he didn't think so.

"Dak was the team dad back in Toronto."

Dak rolled his eyes at Maverick and felt his shoulders droop slightly. Some wingman.

Miranda stared at Maverick, then Dak.

"Everyone needs a dad. You know, someone to talk to," Mav supplied, his knees jiggling, "give you advice, encourage you, guide you. Be there supporting you, no matter what."

Miranda paled as she fiddled with her papers. "Yes, we do."

"I think Dak is the right man to liaise between the players and the hospital, parents, etcetera. He understands schedules, pressures, and how quickly an excited crowd can become too much for a player trying to help someone. He's your guy," Maverick said. "You won't find another man like him."

Miranda gave Dak a look that hinted at fondness. He wanted to believe she'd heard those last few words in a different context. That he might still have a chance with her.

She locked eyes with Dak. "But how will I know if I can trust him?"

. . .

Miranda PRETENDED to study Dak's résumé. Dakarai Morisette. It was crazy how he'd become a candidate for her charity's job opening. She could have hired him without knowing it was *him* if it hadn't been for the charity's chair calling in sick. She skimmed the document, not really reading it, giving herself time to think about Dak and whether she could trust him.

Her gut was saying yes.

Her brain was saying no.

But where her heart wasn't concerned—the job—Dak was likely the right candidate. That was what she needed to focus on right now. She currently had a roster of rookies in need of guidance and who would be more likely to listen to a former player. The team had been losing, and nothing seemed to be going well, especially with the team being slammed in the media thanks to her "crazy ways." Even players such as her loyal team captain, Maverick, who had been forcibly traded off his old team, might decide he'd rather face early retirement than keep on with her if things didn't change soon.

The odds were slim that Dak would make things worse for the team.

And what were the odds of her star player vouching for this candidate—the sexy man she hadn't stopped thinking about since Saturday's lunch date?

Incredibly slim.

So this was meant to be, right?

But she obviously couldn't fully trust Dak. At least not with her heart.

Then again, she didn't have a leg to stand on for not

trusting him. They'd both admitted they had secrets, and they'd both accepted those as their rules.

"Maverick, thank you for meeting with us," Miranda said, standing. She came around her desk to shake his hand goodbye.

She asked Dak, "Do you have some time to stay and chat?"

A roar of tingles raced through her body when he glanced her way, the hope in his gaze igniting her own.

Men. Such trouble. She was in her Slays All Day outfit, and she should be completely immune to tingles. She should not be thinking about this hunk and how he was looking at her like he wanted to be a part of her world.

Maverick gave Dak a smirk as though his friend was about to get slaughtered, then gave Miranda a look that suggested she bring the blade.

When Maverick left, Miranda took his vacated seat beside Dak.

"What is your impression of the Dragons?" she asked. "Be honest."

His mouth immediately opened, but he remained silent for a few beats. Finally, he admitted, "It's a disaster and the team won't last."

Miranda inhaled deeply through her nose, bracing against the surprising pain. It wasn't the first time, or even the hundredth, that she'd heard that. But hearing it from Dak hurt the worst. Even more than from her dad.

"You have a team full of problems," Dak said. "You've inherited and collected some good players, but they're all a mess and it's showing in how they're playing."

She knew that. But for the first time, she truly feared losing her investment. She might have to go to the country club and marry rich if this team didn't find a way to fly within the next year and a half.

Her gut tightened with the promise of failure. She wanted her inheritance to matter. She wanted to add more joy to people's lives. She also wanted to prevent the loss of fortunes men like Gramps had faced. Maybe her family was right and she'd lost sight of reality somewhere along the way and was going about it all wrong.

Miranda nodded to show Dak she'd heard him and knew her team was a mess. "And?" she prompted.

"And," he said with special emphasis, his dark eyes locking on hers, "I'm pretty sure you have a plan. Despite what the media says, you aren't some ditzy heiress thinking it would be fun to own a bunch of hot jocks." He shared a hint of a humorous smile, and she allowed her shoulders to loosen a notch.

"And the charity?"

"It's young. But a good idea. A really good idea. I read the job description and I think I'd be an asset."

"Okay, so let's pretend I'm not some spoiled rich princess trying to feel important or on the lookout for a tax break. What do you think I'm trying to accomplish with this charity?"

His tiny smile turned into a full-fledged grin. "You're gunning for the Stanley Cup through good deeds, obviously."

She grinned back before their former seriousness returned.

Dak continued, "If your players are grounded and focused, and their lives aren't a mess, they'll be more likely to win. There's also the element of team bonding that will develop while working on an important, external goal such as helping a charity."

She nodded, relieved that he hadn't immediately mentioned positive publicity like he thought she was an acknowledgment hound.

"Is this job what you really want?" she asked. "You have a café to run and awards to win."

He stared at her, silent. She watched his expression, the small flickers as he questioned himself, trying to come up with an honest, complete answer.

"How about this?" she said, stacking her hands on top of each other on the armrest closest to him. "Would it be bad for you, personally, to return to the NHL? You'd mentioned wanting to leave this world."

Dak filled his lungs with air, his glorious wide chest expanding under his well-cut white shirt that made him look like a dark and powerful man in all the best ways. He emptied his lungs. "You know, I've been seeking purpose ever since I left the NHL because of my shoulder injury. The café's supposed to fill that hole, and it was my retirement dream. And while I get that it'll take a while for it to fill the void, it's been almost a year."

"How long's a man to wait?" she asked dryly.

"Right?" He paused for a second. "Playing was my dream since I was five years old. That's a long time to stay in a dream." He was silent for a moment, taking in her office, the photos on the walls. She could hear the change in conviction when he resumed speaking. "I believe I was made for hockey. But to answer your question about this opportunity?" His intoxicating, confident, lit-up grin returned. "Ms. Slays All Day, I'm pretty sure this job is what I'm meant to do and that I was made for this job of yours."

She felt her hopes grow and rise like an inflating hot air balloon.

"You're going to face publicity being associated with this team," Miranda warned. "And it likely won't be positive."

"Are you asking me if I'm afraid, or if I'm as loyal and steadfast as Maverick?" Dak locked eyes with her, and it was as if the room shrank around them, the air drawn out along with the square footage.

"Nobody's as loyal as Maverick." That man was like a superglued clam when it came to telling anyone what had really gone down in those almost-career-ending moments in Lafayette. And he wasn't silent because of shame or embarrassment. It was loyalty. "But yes, I'm asking both questions."

"Once you have your people dig around into my past—if you haven't already—you'll find I'm someone you can trust. Early in my career, I didn't always make the best decisions, but there's a good reason Maverick Blades is my best friend."

"Loyalty?"

"I'd like to think we share that trait."

"So I'm guessing you won't fill me in on what happened in Lafayette that got him traded?"

"I'm not at liberty to say."

She smiled. "Then I'll never ask."

"As a member of your charity's team, I'll be loyal. I'll stand up for you and your decisions. I promise you I'll put my heart and soul into this job just like I have every other team I've been on." His eyes searched hers, and she felt the apology as well as the promise. "If you'll have me."

When Dak exited her office, Miranda remained in the floral chair for a long time, her breathing shaky, her thoughts circling, refusing to argue with each other.

Her decisions were already made. No debate needed.

She should be mad at Dak, upset, suspicious, and mistrusting.

And she wasn't.

He'd kept her in the dark, known more than she had, giving him potentially more power in their relationship. But he hadn't abused it and had only done so because he'd been obeying her ground rules.

A reasonable woman would still keep Dak far away from her team and her heart.

She'd never had much patience for being reasonable.

She moved to her desk and picked up her phone. Her assistant answered.

"Is Dak gone?" she asked, knowing he would be.

"Yes."

"That was his job interview for the charity."

"Yes."

"I trust that the file HR brought up for you checked out?" She knew the answer had to be yes, or HR would never have scheduled the interview on behalf of the charity. Dak had passed their dig into his life.

She toyed with her necklace, thinking.

A good boss would read that file herself.

A good potential girlfriend—even a friend—wouldn't.

But she was a boss first. And maybe the only role she'd be playing from now on.

But did it matter whether she read the file if HR had flagged nothing for her? Delegation was a good thing, wasn't it?

"He had some partying days in his rookie years," her assistant said, sounding bored.

"Were they bad?"

"Pretty standard rookie stuff. Nothing human resources was worried about. He's in the running?"

"Yes. He'd be an excellent addition."

Hesitantly, her assistant added, "I overheard that you're dating him?"

So much for keeping that a secret.

"The charity and team need him more than I do. Call the charity's board members, tell them he has my stamp of approval. If they agree he's the winning candidate, call him in three hours and let him know he's hired."

Her heart would have to get over the loss.

CHAPTER 5

*D*ak ensured the back of his shirt was tucked in and his tie was straight as he entered the tastefully decorated, trendy restaurant. Its high ceilings and wide entry with marble walls and oversized planters made him feel as though he was barely average height rather than over six feet tall. Hopefully the meal portion sizes weren't in opposition to the largesse of the entry, or this would be the last time Miranda invited him to a business dinner due to the cost of feeding him his fill.

The maître d' showed him to the table where Miranda was already waiting. For a moment it felt like a date as her eyes connected with his, a flash of joy brightening her expression before she tamped it down and studied her glass of wine.

All about the business. Right. She was now his boss.

He'd accepted the position with her charity and had been working for two and a half weeks with the players and charity board (which included Miranda) as well as the hospital to coordinate how the team could help and support families with sick kids.

It felt good to be back among players. Sure, he wasn't on the ice, but he understood the language of the players. The subtle nuances and body language, letting him know where he was in the pecking order and when he was earning respect.

But the job had created distance between himself and Miranda. He'd go to text her a joke or to say hi, then wonder if it was okay. She wasn't exactly his boss, but she was. He answered to the board, and she was vice-chair. In the few conversations they'd had at work, as soon as the topic turned slightly personal, it got awkward. Neither of them knew what to do or how to act anymore. He wanted to ask her out, but he got the sense she kept her personal and professional life very separate, and he was now on the professional side. And there was no jumping from one side to the other.

At least the new job and his café kept him too busy to think about it much. That and working in the soup kitchen over Thanksgiving. His dog Milo was starting to think he was a stranger.

"Miranda," he said, bending to land a soft kiss on her cheek. He longed to place it on her lips, to linger, to inhale her and hold her. They were going to have to talk about that, because he'd really enjoyed having her in his life. Surely there had to be a way to swing a relationship without stirring any conflict-of-interest pots.

"Dak, how are things? Are you settling in with the job?" She toyed with the stem of her wineglass, her gaze straying from his to dance along his shoulders, his arms.

"Everyone's been awesome. Thank you."

The waiter appeared at his elbow, offering wine. He nodded.

When the waiter left, Dak said, "I was going to order a

Caesar, but I have it on good authority that this isn't where I can get the best one in the city."

Miranda laughed, her shoulders relaxing. She was wearing a serious black skirt and a light cream-colored sweater, its softness echoing the curve of her chest. "True. I checked out their row of awards when I came in, and that one was definitely missing. I wonder who won it?"

They shared a smile over the rims of their wineglasses. Man, he missed her something fierce.

"So what's up?" Dak asked, setting down his glass. The invitation to a suppertime strategy meeting had surprised him. For some reason, he'd expected her to hold all meetings in her offices.

"We're just waiting for the team's public relations rep, the chair of the charity board, and the hospital's publicity director. Everyone has a few ideas on how we can get the players more involved before Christmas hits next month, and this seemed like a good way to lay them all out at once."

Dak nodded.

"I hope I haven't thrown too much at the team this season." She focused on him fully for the first time since he'd sat down.

Dang. Ms. Slays All Day was back. He'd enjoyed seeing that flicker of the old Miranda.

"Most are on board with working with the charity and look forward to it." Players were used to insane schedules. What the rookies weren't used to was the culture shock of their entire existence turning on a dime after they got the call. Personally, he'd gone from overnight bus rides to games with guys cooking ramen in the aisles to first-class plane seats and five-star hotels. It was whiplash going from a nobody to instant fame. Suddenly there was money, comforts, attention. So much attention.

"Well, if you need anything, or sense a disturbance in the force, let me know."

"Star Wars fan?" Dak found his hand slipping across the table to grasp Miranda's and quickly brought it back when she hesitated.

"You're my boss now," he stated. Her expression fell, surprising him.

She rubbed her eyebrow, uncharacteristic stress showing through her Slays All Day demeanor. "I was hoping that you and I..." She smiled sadly. "I need you in the charity."

"You can't have both? Me there as well as here?"

"I..." Her cheeks pinked, and for the first time he saw reservation, uncertainty. It hurt more than he wanted to admit.

"Okay, we'll discuss it later," he said quickly, hoping that wasn't a lie.

"Thank you."

He straightened, adjusted his tie. "I liked the home game pyrotechnics on Monday night."

"Daisy-Mae suggested it."

"And I noticed people were wearing Dragons merchandise and not just throwing it out after it was given to them."

She let out a laugh that sounded painful. The media hadn't been gentle on her lately. The team had an impressive loss ratio, and it felt as if they were running down a track that would never branch off in a different direction. In other words, a win.

The extras spent on the spectator experience hadn't gone unnoticed either. The media piled on her, stating that she'd forgotten what mattered—winning—and was willing to buy her likability with the costly pyrotechnic shows and free home-game merchandise. The press conveniently ignored that the Dragons actually had some social media followers now and had experienced a boost in season ticket sales as a result. Nope, they'd decided she was a rich girl throwing an NHL party where everyone was invited.

"Small steps in the right direction," he said, feeling as though his encouragement was moot against the negativity she and the team faced.

"That's how you climb Everest. One step at a time." She lifted her glass toward him as if to toast, then took a sip.

"I'm going to be at Maverick's on the weekend. He needs some help fixing some plaster. Wanna come help? We might need to sledgehammer something and that's always fun."

She shook her head. "I'm pretty sure Maverick's ranch is his women-free zone."

It was true, but he was willing to break his friend's rule for Miranda.

"How long have the two of you known each other?"

"Since our Toronto days. Will you be in Sweetheart Creek for some downtime this weekend?"

She nodded.

"Well, if you want to grab a coffee…"

"I'll be there Friday night through to Sunday night. I can make you supper one of those nights if you aren't busy. And maybe we can talk about us?" She leaned forward, that familiar softer Miranda shining through.

He could see the moment she caught herself, and she leaned back, clearing her throat. Her heart had overwritten her brain and its plans, and she'd once again invited him into her personal space, her retreat from the world.

He felt like fist pumping the air in celebration.

Dak leaned over the table, asking quietly, "Just one of the nights?"

He was rewarded with a laugh that kept his spirits buoyed for the entire evening.

ALL DURING THE dinner meeting Miranda marveled at how calm Dak was. He was well-spoken as he pointed out possible pitfalls in their charity's plans, problem-solving on the go as they ironed out ways they could ensure that the sick kids they were helping didn't look like they were being used as publicity props.

She couldn't date this man and risk blowing up the work he was doing for the charity. She needed him there. The players and kids needed him.

Her heart did, too, but sadly it was used to not getting its way.

By the time the meeting ended, her patience and confidence had been exhausted, even though things had gone better than she'd hoped. Miranda felt crazy for starting a team charity when the Dragons couldn't even win a game. Maybe she should be allowing more ice time for the players rather than splitting their focus.

As she stood in the cool, late November air waiting for her car to be brought around, she felt a presence beside her. She turned, already smiling before she fully registered that the man beside her was Dak.

"Doubting your very existence yet?" he asked jovially, his hands deep in his suit pants pockets.

She rolled her eyes and did a little arm flap, like she was having a meltdown. Or as her mother would say, causing a scene. But Dak laughed, sharing the moment.

"They made me doubt myself in ways only my family has succeeded in doing."

"No," Dak said in disbelief, studying her.

She smiled wanly, that familiar warming in her gut spreading through her as she took him in. He was tall, handsome, and commanding. Women entering the restaurant slowed to rake their gazes over him while men eyed him with suspicion, holding their wives a little closer when Dak smiled back.

Across the street, a squirrel scuttled up a tree along the edge of the San Antonio Riverwalk, and Miranda found herself wishing Dak would take her hand and lead her down the walkway. This time of night, under the strings of lights, crossing small bridges under the shadows of large trees, it would be romantic. An escape from their day, the pressures of making the right decisions, and a juxtaposition from the bustling city towering behind them.

"I admire your conviction," Dak said, breaking their silence.

"My conviction?"

"Yeah. You know what'll help your players, your community, the kids, and the hospital, and you aren't afraid to shake things up within the establishment. You're good for these men." He was eyeing her from the side, and she felt the power of his words, his support.

"Which men?"

He chuckled. "I'm pretty sure each and every one that you encounter."

"I appreciate it," she whispered. She stared across the street, still wishing he'd take her hand, break her rules, and insist they continue to date even though she was his boss. That he'd ensure everything would turn out okay, and that nobody would dare suggest she'd hired him because of romantic nepotism.

And yet she'd accidentally invited him over on the weekend. And he'd accepted. They were practically asking the press to discover them, then skewer them with some crazy conflict of interest that didn't exist.

"I appreciate how you helped me get my message across in there," she said.

"They see the value. It's just more work, more scheduling of their already busy players. It probably feels like one more thing, and right now they're consumed with getting a win so they don't lose their careers."

"It's just so frustrating!" She turned to Dak, wanting to pound her frustration out on the sidewalk with her heels.

"They'll get there. And that's why you have me. To talk to the players, the board, the hospital, the families."

"Thank you."

It was taking her car a long time to arrive, but she didn't mind. She wanted to stretch this moment, spend more time with Dak.

"The toughest part is patience," he said.

She sighed, and he placed a hand on her arm, turning them so they were facing. She held her breath, certain a kiss was going to happen.

If it was, she should stop it, right?

He dropped a kiss on her cheek, and she leaned against it, inhaling his aroma, his strength, hating how much she wished that kiss had landed on her lips.

She opened her eyes, stepping back, trying to create distance so she didn't do something stupid that could hurt him should someone take a photo and publish it under a nasty headline.

"For the record," he murmured, "you're not letting me go."

"We work together."

"I know."

"It wouldn't be smart to get involved."

"You haven't forgiven me for not fessing up that I knew who you were?"

"It's not that."

"Then what is it?"

"I don't want to hurt you."

"Ma'am," the valet said, startling her. Her car had arrived, and the valet moved to hold her car door open.

The valet stepped aside as Dak, cradling her elbow, led her to her waiting car.

"We'll finish this conversation this weekend, then?" he said, his voice low.

"Until the weekend," she whispered loud enough for him to hear before he closed her door.

As Miranda drove off, watching Dak grow smaller in her mirror, she wondered how she was going to balance dating him with not destroying his credibility with the team, the charity, and with the press. Because he didn't deserve that.

But she also didn't deserve to give up the one man who'd caught her attention and admiration in years.

CHAPTER 6

*E*ven before Dak reached Miranda's small house outside of Sweetheart Creek, he was spent. He should be at his café, serving Friday night drinks alongside the woman he'd promoted to manager. He'd spent more than forty hours there during the week training staff to take over for him, and another forty at the rink talking to players about the roles they wanted within the charity—if any—and he was wiped out.

And yet, instead of steering his car toward Gingerbread Café to help with the evening rush or taking his dog home after spending hours at the rink with him, he took the overpass that led to the highway, leaving the city behind. The closer he got to Miranda's, the more his shoulders relaxed but the more antsy he felt.

He wanted to date her, however that happened to fit into their busy lives. But he also didn't want to bring more drama to her life, and their relationship would surely draw criticism as well as skepticism as to why he'd been added to the charity team.

He'd already been singled out by the press, already noted to have the same atypical philosophy toward Miranda's player care as she held. Normally, it would be good to be on the same page as your employer, but in this case, the reporters were unrelenting.

He could handle anything they threw at him about a relationship with Miranda, but could the charity? Could Miranda?

As he stopped in her driveway, smiling at the small, honest looking abode, her sister's words from the elevator came to mind. Her family thought Miranda was losing her mind for wanting a simple life and for escaping it all. Dak thought it was admirable.

In the passenger seat beside him sat Milo, his medium-sized mutt, tongue lolling to the side as he took in the new scenery. Dak hoped Miranda didn't mind a four-legged date-crasher.

Not that this was officially a date. But he'd like it to be. He hoped they'd unwind together, just two people being themselves in a house so small they couldn't lose each other. Because if she let him, he planned to spend as many moments as he could cherishing her, sliding his arm around her shoulders and sitting close so he could soak in her fiery presence like a balm.

Dak hopped out of his car, holding his door open as a signal to Milo that he could come too. The duo inhaled the fresh country air before Milo zipped across the yard, a light gray and brown blur as he followed scents brought out by a recent rain. The forlorn sound of cattle calling to each other in the distance filled the air, and Milo's head popped up and he gave a soft whine.

Dak patted the side of his leg, whistling. The dog, reluctant to give up the trail he was following, obeyed.

"Nice spot, hey buddy?" Dak said, rubbing the dog's ears. "You have to be on your very best behavior. This woman is important. Got it?"

Milo panted happily, and Dak grinned as he wound his way through a small garden path that smelled of roses, lit up with solar lights as dusk settled in around him.

He set his phone on silent as he walked. He'd chatted with Landon, the team's goalie, aka The Blockade, during the drive. He was a former teammate who'd been traded to the Dragons after a shattered ankle had been slow to heal. Yesterday Dak had tried to convince him to help with the charity, but Landon had been worried that getting involved might make Cassandra, his new girlfriend who happened to have a son in the program, think he was too involved too soon.

Dak had mentally crossed Landon off the list until tonight's call. The Blockade was in, his hopes up that he could help Cass as well as his team by putting his focus beyond himself and the steady losses.

Getting the team's goalie on board felt huge, and the idea that Dak's work might help the team—and therefore Miranda —sent a swirl of emotion through him.

It felt like he might be the right man, in the right place, about to win it all. Maybe even Miranda's heart.

The sound of the front door closing echoed across the quiet yard, and he looked over his shoulder, already smiling. His dog scrambled up the steps to greet Miranda in her oversized sweater, arms crossed against the chill coming in from the east. She petted the dog, saying nothing, opening her arms as Dak's long legs took up the space between them. He threw his arms around her, holding her like she was a piece of driftwood in a flood, the only thing that could keep him afloat as he gave her a kiss filled with everything in his heart.

"So when do you want to talk about us?" Dak asked Miranda as they washed the dinner dishes at her sink. She froze, stealing a glimpse of his expression. The light above the counter cast shadows across his face, but she could see the curiosity, the desire. The willingness to pursue her despite the wall of professionalism she'd erected between them over the past several weeks.

Supper had been surprisingly quiet but comfortable, his dog giving the odd sigh as he dozed at Dak's feet. Their hands had been entwined on the tabletop as they ate their pumpkin ravioli and Casear salad, and the silence had felt very different from that of her family dinners growing up, where the silence was born out of simmering anger.

That kiss when he'd first arrived... By the time they'd come up for air she could barely recall her name and whose porch they were standing on. There was something between them. Something big. No question.

"So?" Dak prompted, leaning against the counter to give her one of those smiles that crinkled the skin around his eyes and warmed her right down to her toes.

"What are we—how would we handle something like this?" she asked as she pulled the sink plug, sending the tomato-sauce-stained water swirling. "There will be publicity." She took a deep breath. She was talking like a relationship was a sure thing. "*Is* there going to be an us?"

"Yes."

She nodded, squelching the thrill that zipped through her like a current. She felt partly relieved and partly afraid of the certainty of his answer. It was shocking how quickly Dak had become part of her life, her inner circle. She assumed he would be there for her, and vice versa. She'd spent weeks denying him, but in the back of her mind she'd never once stopped thinking about him.

"The press wasn't kind to you this week," he said when she focused on wiping down the sink so she wouldn't have to face him and could think clearly.

"You saw that, huh?"

"I did."

"That's part of the dating Miranda Fairchild package, I'm afraid to say."

"I'm used to it."

She shot him a frown. "Are not."

"You're worth it."

"I need you with the charity." He'd mentioned Landon's change of heart, and she knew how big that was. She also knew that was directly attributable to him and his work.

"Is that the only thing you need me for?" Dak was leaning over the counter now so he could see her better.

Fine. He wanted the truth in all its painful glory? She pivoted to face him.

"You know I'd love to date you."

"Then date me. I already told you I'll go as your plus-one to the charity's gala."

She hesitated. Taking Dak as her date was literally the only thing about the December gala she was looking forward to.

She shook her head, brushing off her thoughts. "You don't know what it'll be like dating me. With the press."

"And you don't know what it's like being with me. All the adoring, drooling women. It's hard to take. Especially when I'm in a tuxedo."

He was teasing her, making light of it.

"Dak. The press can be cruel. You don't—"

"I do know. I've even experienced a taste of it when my marriage broke down. I've watched Maverick navigate it. People don't start dating because they know everything about each other and how it'll all turn out. They date to discover. And I think I'm a good choice because I have a clue what I'm getting into, the strength to endure it, and the wiles to charm those dirty bloodsuckers." He leaned closer, the familiar scent of freshly ground coffee and gingerbread filling her senses.

"It's better if nobody knows. I don't want anyone attacking your credibility. Especially not this early in the charity's life."

"Is that the only reason you want to hide me?"

"Yes," she said with a hint of impatience. "I can't handle it if the press is cruel to you. And I can't cope with the possible threat of you abandoning me and the charity."

"You don't think I'm strong enough?"

"I don't think my allure is strong enough." She felt shaky inside, fearful for revealing her vulnerability.

His hand settled over hers, stopping its movement of wiping things down. It was large, warm, all-encompassing. His breath whispered over her neck as he stood behind her.

"I love that you don't judge the craziness of my life," she said, not looking up, focusing on their clasped hands. "You make me feel normal, and as though my crazy purpose isn't so crazy. Is it wrong to want to protect that?"

"We belong together." The deep timbre of his voice sent tremors through her body. He turned her to face him. "And for the record, I think your allure is plenty strong. There are a lot of reasons to run away, and yet here I am."

"Is it because I'm rich?" she teased, uncomfortable with the intensity of her feelings. It felt like he might stay, be a true partner, and lift her up and not leave. She could actually have a shot with Dak. A long, happily ever after kind of shot.

"I'm rich, too."

"Are you?"

"Stinkingly so."

"Maybe we could swap investment tips."

He chuckled softly. "Yeah? I start cafés I don't want to run, and you buy teams about to go belly up."

"Hm. When you put it that way..." She wound her arms around his shoulders.

He kissed her nose. "Wanna know a secret?"

She nodded.

"I'm glad you're doing things your way with the team. Sometimes old boys' club organizations need a feminine touch."

She raised her eyebrows, stiffening in his embrace. He continued quickly, as though to ward off an upcoming misinterpretation of his words. "I'm just saying that it isn't common to have someone dedicated to taking care of the soft stuff on a pro sports team. You care. A lot. It's a good thing."

Her mother was always telling her she needed to be softer. Less competitive. Less driven. Less...*her*.

"I'm not that soft and caring."

"Miranda." Dak pulled her close. "It's okay to bring some femininity to the boardroom." He laughed at her expression, holding her in front of him before hugging her with those glorious arms. "You're looking at me like I've insulted you."

"Well...calling me soft and caring and making it sound like a compliment while I know I'm being a fiery pain in the butt and going where no woman has gone before... It's an adjustment."

"The NHL might be a family, but it's never had a mom—"

She pulled back and glowered at him.

"I am *not* a mom!"

He laughed and squeezed her so she couldn't escape his arms. "Just so you know, moms are the secret superpower behind all levels of hockey. If it wasn't for moms, we'd all be Neanderthals on the ice, beating each other over the head with our sticks."

"Oh, I've seen how many hockey sticks a team goes through. I'm not so sure y'all are over your Neanderthal stage." The first time she went over the books with the accountant and saw the huge stick order, she thought it was an error.

Dak chuckled at her tone, but instead of riling her up, she felt understood, safe, and she rested her head against his chest, listening to his heartbeat.

"Moms are the people we can count on. The ones who will hug us even when we insist we're too old. They're the ones who miraculously drum up a meal, who show up at every game, who get up even when it's minus thirty and drive us to the rink, hours before the sun would even dare reveal its sunny face. Moms are the backbone of hockey. They do the fundraising, the schedule juggling, they book the hotels, pack the lunches, and spend hours on the road. I don't know how they do it."

"And I'm that? A…mom?"

He gave her such an affectionate smile she couldn't help but feel his words for what they were. A compliment. A sincere one.

And, she couldn't help but think, that if he was the team dad and she was the team mom…

No, it was best to avoid that tempting line of thought in case she got her hopes up too high.

"You're doing good things for your team. These players have been through a lot of uncertainty, but they know you have their back. And your charity is much needed. For all involved."

He finally released her. "But enough about hockey. Tell me a bit about why you chose this house in the middle of cowboy country."

"So you can call me crazy?"

"For all the strange things you do, have I ever once used that word?" His eyebrows were dancing. He was mischievous, handsome, and somehow had just wormed his way even further into her inner trust circle rather than getting the preemptive, protective boot out of it.

"That's right, I haven't," he said, answering for her. He placed a sweet kiss on her lips. "I have it on good authority that there's some really delicious peach cobbler in town. Wanna go on a dessert date?"

For a moment Dak thought Miranda was going to shoot him down, suggest they keep their budding romance completely under wraps and stay in all night.

But she swung out of the kitchen, calling behind her, "Am I driving or are you? Because I love a man who thinks about dessert more than I do."

His dog began barking, dancing after her, ready to go wherever she went. Dak felt the same way.

He laughed and raced after them. "All these years of restricting my diet." He patted his flat stomach as he caught up with her at the door. "I'm making up for lost desserts. But one of these days, it's going to catch up with me."

Miranda slung her arms around his waist in the entryway,

hugging him. "Don't worry. You'll still be a hottie no matter how much cobbler you have."

"I'm holding you to that when I have a paunch."

"Yeah, yeah." She swung her keychain's ring around on the end of her finger, and he snagged it from her.

"I'll drive. you can put your keys away." He watched for her reaction. "I am your boyfriend. And even though it sounds old-fashioned, they get to drive. Especially when they go on dates." His heart was beating like he'd managed a breakaway. He was racing down the ice, not wanting to check behind him, fearing he'd get caught by a defenseman before he could hook the puck past the goalie.

Miranda hesitated, her hand outstretched for her keys. She'd been about to fight, compete. Drive.

Instead, she pulled her goalie, let him by. She dropped her hand.

"But we have to keep things, you know…quiet."

"How quiet?"

"Your reputation matters to me."

"You can't taint this," he teased. He caught her expression and realized she was hesitant because she likely couldn't take more flack. She'd reached her damage limit, and she felt responsible for any negative impact she might cause him or her team.

He gently cupped her chin. "Like I said earlier, you're worth it."

"Dak—"

"Shh. I'm serious. I know what I'm getting into and I can handle it."

"You deserve better than what they might say."

"And so do you. We're in this together." He dangled the

keys, offering them. She glanced at them, then back at him, her expression somber.

"You can drive. But no kissing or hugging or making moon eyes at me." She laughed at his stricken look. "In public. Here you can kiss me all you like."

He swept her into his arms, giving her a long kiss as he slowly let her back down again. "I'm not sure that will carry me through dessert. Better kiss me again."

She complied, and he kissed her long and slow until her body was completely relaxed in his arms. When he tried to pull away, she snagged his lips between her teeth, and the kiss grew deeper again as they moved against the wall for support.

Miranda knew how to kiss, and he avoided thinking about where she might have received the experience. He wanted to be her only one. From here on out and until forever. Her last first kiss.

She tangled her fingers in his short hair, and he kissed her neck, just about getting a crick in his own. Kissing her tonight, he realized she wasn't nearly as tall as his perception. He moved them toward the stairs, lifting her in his arms, and she laughed against his lips.

He set her down on the bottom step so she was closer to his height. "You thought I was going to do something else, didn't you?"

"Maybe."

"Maybe later. Right now, I'm just trying to save our necks." He kissed her slow and deep again before escorting her out the door, dazed and out of breath.

He could get used to kissing Miranda Fairchild just like that.

· · ·

ON SWEETHEART CREEK'S Main Street, there were a few pickup trucks parked here and there, but it was mostly empty at this time of night. At the saloon, a brown dog ducked under the swinging doors and onto the sidewalk, wagging his tail and carrying a piece of cheese bread like a well-earned trophy.

Dak hurried around to Miranda's side of the car after he parked in front of the diner. He held the door as she climbed out. Milo had come for the ride and had sighed as though feeling put out at having to sit in the back, a sign Miranda appreciated as it suggested there weren't a lot of women in Dak's life ousting the dog from riding shotgun.

"Stay," Dak commanded Milo. The dog lay down on the back seat, chin on his paws.

"He's really good," Miranda remarked.

"Yeah, but I worry that he's lonely with me working so many hours right now—even with a dog walker."

The next closest vehicle was a truck several spots down. It had a large veterinarian box in the back, and a man with dark hair and blue eyes was holding a puppy. When he saw Dak and Miranda, he called, "Missing a dog?"

Miranda shook her head.

"Need one?" the man joked, ruffling the puppy's fur, letting loose a cloud of dust. "This little one looks like she might be in need of a home."

Dak hesitated, his eyes on the skinny, wriggling puppy. "It's a sign," he whispered to Miranda.

"He already has a dog," Miranda called, trying to steer Dak toward the diner. "Two dogs doesn't solve your time problem."

"Milo would have company."

"Milo might act out, and puppies need a lot of training."

"What about you? You need a dog? For security?"

"Nice try."

"Milo needs a friend," Dak said, edging toward the puppy. "And this puppy needs a home."

The man at the truck shifted the puppy in his arms, and the dog stretched, trying to take the man's cowboy hat. The man took it in stride as he extended his right hand to Dak, causing him to close the distance.

"Brant Wylder. I run the local vet clinic as well as help any strays."

And before Miranda knew it, the puppy was in Dak's arms, and only a few minutes later promises were being made around the dog's possible adoption.

Miranda watched Dak and the puppy with longing. She wished she had the kind of life where she could have a dog as well as the time to train it.

But she did seem to be having some luck with feeding the skinny stray cat she saw slipping through her yard from time to time. Maybe one day it would let her pet him.

Brant was asking Dak about his schedule, and Miranda said, "Don't worry, he has people to train and take care of his pets. He's not a normal mortal like the rest of us."

"You're normal?" Dak said, laughing so loud he frightened the puppy. He leaned over, giving her an affectionate nudge. Then he handed the puppy back to Brant with a promise to be in touch.

"You know," she said quietly, "if you asked the arena, I'm pretty sure a puppy could come in with you. As long as it's housebroken. And maybe you could get her certified as a therapy animal and take her to the hospital."

"My wife can help with certification," Brant added.

Dak winked at Miranda. "And don't worry about the rink. Milo will show the pup the ropes."

Miranda's mouth dropped open. "You're already bringing your dog to work!"

"Just here and there."

"And you think I'm sassy!"

"I do." He was grinning.

As they said goodbye to the puppy, Miranda realized that just like her man had fallen in love with the dog, she'd fallen in love with him.

CHAPTER 7

The following Sunday, Dak got the full tour of the gardens surrounding Miranda's Sweetheart Creek home after helping Maverick fix a few things around his money pit of a house—as well as thoroughly mocking him for his hideous taste in shower curtains. The guy needed an interior decorator. And maybe a whole new house. During the season players didn't get much time off, and it appeared his buddy Mav was spending most of it taking aggressive renovation action on his little farmhouse. Which meant he was inwardly fuming over what had gone down in Lafayette a year ago. Or in love.

Dylan O'Neill, the team's injured center, had come out to help despite the cast on his foot. Landon Jackson and Leo Pattra had come to lend a hand as well.

Dak felt good, and he rolled his right shoulder, checking it for stiffness or aches. It had been nice to do something with the guys to help keep his mind off his secret relationship with Miranda.

How long would they have to stay silent? Forever? Until the team started to win? Until they got tired of each other?

The last one wasn't going to happen. Miranda was all he thought about from dawn to dusk. If anyone hacked into their text messages, it would be abundantly clear they were an item. He'd finally found a use for the heart emoticon. Not that he made rampant use of it or anything. He was still a man, after all, but as his sister Nia would say, he was crushing hard.

Dak took Miranda's hand, admiring her late bloom of roses, a few birds swooping overhead as the sun slowly set.

"How's Landon doing?" she asked. "I heard his girlfriend's son lives on a ranch nearby and has some heart issues?"

"Landon's okay, and Dusty will be, too."

Miranda had paused to hear the answer, and now she turned, placing one hand gently on Dak's forearm in a sweet gesture that felt like a piece of home.

"I'm glad."

"You care a lot about your team, don't you?" he asked. "Why is that?" Most owners cared, but this felt different.

She scrunched her nose and shook her head, sending a tendril of dark hair sliding out of its confines within her ponytail.

"You can tell me," he said, tucking the strands behind her ear.

She was silent for another long moment, then said, "This team is my grandfather's. It's his real legacy."

"I didn't realize. Everyone says it's your team."

"It is."

She began walking, her head lowered, brow furrowed in thought, the leisurely pace from earlier now gone. The garden tour seemed to be over as she headed toward the fence that separated the edge of her yard and driveway from the neighbor's pasture.

"My grandparents on my mom's side didn't grow up with much. Before Gramps met Grams, he made it into the NHL during college."

"Really?" How did Dak not know Miranda had NHL roots?

"Suddenly, he went from a struggling scholarship student who had nothing to a man making as much as the chief of police just for stepping onto the ice. Gramps didn't know what to do with the money, the fame, or any of it, really. He spent it all, shattered his ankle, and then was dropped from the team. He ended up declaring bankruptcy, and he hadn't yet finished his education. In a lot of ways, he was worse off than before, especially when his ankle didn't heal properly and he couldn't pick up manual labor jobs."

Miranda stopped at the fence, the long pasture grass beside her swaying like something was moving through it. The wind gusted, and her hair broke free from behind her ear again, waving, taunting him to try and restrain it.

"It's not something the family talks about. I think Gramps was ashamed by how the money changed him, how much he and Grams struggled because of his actions."

"It's a common story."

"When Gramps met Grams, he was broke and at his lowest. He was embarrassed because he knew he could've offered her a different life if he'd managed his finances and hadn't acted like fame and fortune would last forever. He could have bought her the ring he wanted instead of finding one at a pawnshop, having it polished, and hoping she didn't realize it had been part of someone else's broken dreams."

"And you want to prevent your grandfather's story from

happening to others," Dak stated, the pieces of the Miranda puzzle falling into place. The life coaches and the financial experts guiding her players.

"It had been his dream to go back somehow."

"Really?" he asked, turning to face her in surprise.

"He didn't mention it to anyone, but one afternoon he told me his story, and I could tell he wanted a do-over. So when I got the trust fund from my dad's parents, I knew immediately what to put it toward."

The grass rustled in front of them and a light brown cat appeared before diving back in. Miranda crouched and made soft clicking sounds. The grass stirred, but the cat didn't reappear.

"He's been gone for over a decade. It sounds silly, me buying a team for him," Miranda said, her cheeks flushing.

"Not at all."

"And the charity..." She licked her lips, her shoulders drooping as she stood again, the cat coming to peek at her from behind the fence post.

"Personal reasons?" he supplied.

She looked sad, and he pulled her close.

"Sorry, I just can't help imagining what my grandparents went through."

"They had a sick kid?"

She nodded. "Their first born. They did everything they could to save him. The medical bills decimated their shaky financial situation even further. Rags to riches, to rags and even more rags." Miranda looked up at him from within the cocoon of his arms. "I know how risky it is to run a team. Especially in Texas." Her voice had gone low, and he pulled her closer. "I just couldn't help but think if somebody had been there showing Gramps how to take care of his future, then maybe it could have been different. There was always a part of him that seemed broken, and I think it held him back from having the life he wanted in so many ways. I wanted to do something good with my inheritance from my other grandfather."

Her voice grew soft, hesitant in a way he hadn't heard before. "My dad doesn't approve. He thinks my grandfather—his dad—would have found my actions foolish and unnecessarily risky. He worked hard for the money he left for me, and I fear I'll lose it all."

Dak reached for her hand, cool from the evening breeze. He slipped his fingers between hers, locking them together. With his other hand, he gently held her chin.

"I believe in what you're doing."

Her eyes welled and her lower lip trembled.

"It *is* foolish though," she said, her voice shaking. "I'm being pushy with my players. They could hire their own financial advisors if they wanted them."

"But they won't. Trust me." Seeing her disbelief, he chuckled, trying to cajole her into a more hopeful mood, one where she rebounded with confidence and conviction. "How many jocks do you know who'll ask for help because they have too much money?" He made her look at him, see the truth in his words, borrow his faith since hers was faltering. "Who is going to put up their hand and say, 'Uh, what do I do with all of this dope cash?' Most of us spend it because we understand how to live with an empty bank account. We spent years waiting for the call, living from crappy check to crappy check. Some of us were on teams that couldn't even afford to pay us what we were owed. A person isn't born with the skills or with role models to show us how to invest in our futures. We just see everyone throwing money at us like its confetti that will never end, and the guy at the locker beside us is buying everything he can get his hands on." He lowered his voice, coaxing her. "Trust your gut. These guys need these skills, and they need a charity to get behind. This is the right direction."

She gave a shaky laugh. "I hope so, because getting laughed at is growing old."

She was about to slip out of his arms, but he held her closer, gently lowering his lips to hers. "You can lean on me anytime. For pep talks or hugs and kisses. In private or in public."

"Thanks."

He could see her slowly returning to her strong and confident persona again, covering up those thin cracks she kept so carefully hidden.

"How do you do it?" he asked as they walked back to the house where pie and a movie awaited.

"Do what?"

"How do you keep going when everything looks and feels like a colossal disaster?"

Miranda stared at him for a beat, a shadow of fear flickering across her olive complexion before she gave him a slight smile.

"I feel it," she said quietly and with a visible serene assurance. "Right here." She made a fist and placed it knuckles-first against her chest.

"Feel what, exactly?"

"Certainty. A certain knowledge that it'll all work out. That we'll have a winning team in a few short years."

ON MONDAY MORNING, Miranda was at her desk thinking about Dak. She was still a bit surprised she'd told him her grandparents' story and revealed her fears. Deanna didn't even know the entire tale. So why had she shared it with Dak?

Because he was all kinds of awesome, that was why. He understood things her family didn't, and she was starting to dream dangerously—of love, of marriage. All the big things.

Her office door opened. Her assistant poked his head through the doorway. "Meeting. Taking it in the conference room?"

"Yes." She gathered her leather folder as she stood.

"Did you hear the news?" Jeremy asked, waiting for her by the door.

She quirked her head. There was a lot he could be referring to. That her mom had changed her hair color. (Yawn.) That the feral cat outside her place in Sweetheart Creek had let her share part of her muffin with him from afar on Sunday evening. (Yes!) That their right wing's wife had given birth to their first child. (Aw.) That their team couldn't seem to summon a win this month. (No words for that one.)

"Lafayette fired their coaches."

She froze. "All of them? Right now? Mid-season?"

Jeremy nodded.

"Why? Because they're on a losing streak as bad as ours?"

He nodded again.

She let out a huff. "Well, I doubt firing everyone will help. Their owner is a real Class A..." She inhaled, her mother's words coming to mind about being a lady. "You know what I was going to say," she muttered. He gave a joyful grin as she left her office, bouncing along after her.

She entered the boardroom, and before she sat, she announced to her managers and coaches, "Lafayette fired their coaching team. They're going to be a mess on Wednesday night when we play them. But we can't assume they'll hand us a win." She gestured to Jeremy to pour coffee for everyone as she took her seat. Before the men sitting at the table could tell her to skip tomorrow's charity work with their players so they could squeeze in an extra practice, she continued, "It's time to put all of your crazy ideas on the table, because we're winning a game in two days' time."

CHAPTER 8

On Tuesday morning after practice, several of the Dragons met at the Cho Memorial Children's Hospital for their first visit.

Dak had coordinated some activities for the players and children to do together, and Miranda hadn't seen so many smiles in one place in a very long time. She didn't think the ward had ever been that noisy or full of fun.

And maybe a little competitive as well. He'd designed a few games the kids could compete in with their designated Dragon—things such as wheelchair races where their personal NHL player was their "reindeer" while they rode in the "sleigh" as Santa. There was a simple obstacle course down the hallway, and kids dropped a wrapped gift under a large Christmas tree in the common area to "win."

There was also the tongue depressor and cotton ball hockey game where the massive men crowded around each other, fighting over the cotton ball with their tongue depressors, struggling to make a goal into a tipped-over pill cup. Landon, the team's goalie, kept announcing he was in goal no matter which cup the players were aiming for. The kids thought his scurrying around trying to make saves was hilarious—especially when his socks slid out from under him and he took dramatic spills. The kids played referee and were ruthless about the rules, which changed without notice. Miranda was pretty sure the players wanted to get called on penalties by the sixteen sets of eyes watching their every move.

When things got too wound up, Dak moved swiftly into some one-on-one time to prevent the kids from over-exerting themselves. The nurses quietly helped and guided, as did some visiting parents. Even they were smiling. And some were flirting, too, which Miranda couldn't blame them for. There was nothing as sexy as a grown man getting into a silly game for the benefit of making a child smile.

Dak had brought a supply of storybooks, sticker books, hockey cards, and crafts, the kids choosing which they'd like to do with their player for the last half of the one-hour visit.

Miranda stood in the doorway where Dak was reading a story to a girl who was recovering from a skin graft on her foot after a terrible burn. He sat in the chair by Reese's bed, showing her the illustrations. The five-year-old leaned over the edge of her bed, resting her curly head on Dak's shoulder, and he shifted closer, making her more comfortable.

As they got close to the end of their story, an alarm caused Miranda to jump. She shot Dak a panicked look, then checked the sensors hooked up to the child.

"Fire," Dak mouthed, scooping the small child into his arms.

"That's a fire alarm!" Reese shrieked, her terror thickening the air.

"Wait!" Miranda quickly untangled Reese's sensors,

unplugging them from the machine by her bed. She eyed the door, afraid they were breaking protocols, and by evacuating without permission they'd be more hinderance than help.

"We go," Dak said, eyeing the panicking girl in his arms. Miranda nodded and stepped aside.

"Watch her foot," she said, wishing she could put a bubble around Reese to ensure she didn't get bumped as the commotion in the hallway increased.

"They're probably just testing the alarms," Dak said calmly but loudly, trying to be heard over the child's crying and the alarm, his legs already taking large strides down the hall. Nurses hustled, faces pinched, crisscrossing hallways, emergency procedures in action.

They weren't testing alarms.

"Where do we go?" Miranda asked, scanning the hallway for smoke or flames. A passing nurse pointed to the station at the ward's entrance. Another nurse stood with a clipboard, checking off patients as staff wheeled or walked them out. So many children were still in their beds, and Miranda's players stood in room doorways waiting for direction.

Elevators. Fire. These kids needed to be carried down the stairs.

To Dak she said, "Take her to the muster area. I'm going to round up the team and more kids."

She turned, but all of the jerseyed men had already left their doorways, following Dak's lead. Soon they were streaming from the rooms, children in their arms or pushing wheelchairs or entire beds in some cases. Nurses swarmed them, calling out directions.

After what felt like half an hour but had been less than five minutes according to the clock at the ward's entrance,

Miranda found herself outside, standing in the bright sunshine surrounded by people.

"I'm going back in," the nurse beside her said, shoving an armload of blankets into Miranda's arms and pointing her toward the gathered groups of children and players. "Keep everyone out here."

It was quite the sight, these big men with sick children in their arms, looking like mother hens, fussing and soothing patients they'd met only forty-five minutes ago as fire trucks screamed in the distance.

Miranda handed out blankets, then joined Dak, Reese still in his arms, the child's panic easing. "Everything okay? What can I do?"

"Just stay out here, I think." He gestured with his chin toward a group of nurses hustling around the parking lot, organizing, calming children and parents, and doing what they could to ensure comfort.

"Let's get everyone in a circle on the grass," Miranda said to her players, pointing to a green area between two parking sections. Despite it being a little more than two weeks until Christmas, it was fairly warm, barely even sweatshirt weather. "I think this would be a great time to hear some real-life NHL stories, don't you?"

Dak rocked and shushed Reese as he walked, whispering to her as she slowly shuddered and relaxed, her tears subsiding. Miranda's heart sighed as she watched. She was definitely in love with this man.

Once everyone was in the circle, Dak began telling them a story from his NHL days when he and Landon used to play together.

"So we're all standing there, looking around. There's maybe fifty seconds left on the clock and we can't find the puck. It's nowhere! This player on the other team was getting mad at Landon—he plays goal in case he hasn't told you that already."

Landon gave a sheepish wave, and the kids laughed and pointed.

"Anyway, because we're up a goal, this guy thinks Landon's hidden the puck so we can play out the clock and win. Basically, make it so there's not enough time left in the game for the other team to score a point and send us into overtime. And *everyone* knows that when Landon plays in Calgary, his grandma's making us all an amazing post-game feast. And you never keep Grandma waiting."

"That's true," Landon said seriously.

"And then guess what? There's this kid pointing and yelling and banging on the glass that separates the stands from the ice. I thought maybe *he* had the puck somehow. But, no, he's pointing at the ref. So we're all looking at the referee like he took the puck? That makes no sense."

"Did he steal it?" a kid asked.

"Turns out the puck got stuck in his skate! It got wedged in between the blade and the boot of the skate. Can you believe it? We're standing there lost, and it's literally under his foot."

"And the good news was that I didn't get beat up by that Calgary player," Landon said. "That was nice."

"And no overtime," Dak added.

"Happy grandma," Landon said, rubbing his stomach as though recalling the feast.

Dak grew silent, looking down at Reese who had snuggled in and appeared to be fast asleep in his arms, her bandaged foot sticking out from under the blanket Dak had spread over her.

The stories continued, the laughter and smiles never stopped.

This moment, right here, was worth everything.

Miranda locked eyes with Dak and mouthed thank you. He gave her a nod, his own expression mirroring the gratitude she felt for this group that was becoming like a family, their warmth and support extending to everyone present. She never wanted today to end.

THE DRAGONS WALKED the few blocks from the hospital to the Gingerbread Café. Dak walked beside Miranda, wishing he could hold her hand in public.

It had felt good being useful though, and to be in the right place at the right time, doing something meaningful. It had also been a successful start to their charity work.

There had been a small, isolated fire in the hospital, but everyone was okay and the damage to the cafeteria was minimal.

In his café, with the twinkling Christmas lights strung along the back wall, Dak settled himself behind the large coffee bar and began serving up various drinks and snacks with the help of his wide-eyed staff. They knew he used to play and was now working with the Dragons' charity, but they'd likely never believed nearly half of the team would be in their shop asking for low-fat, no-whip lattes.

"Do you need help?" Miranda asked, looking as though she was willing to leap over the bar and get her hands dirty.

"Do I ever ask to get behind your desk?" he asked.

"No, you just come back there and start bossing me around."

He recalled coming behind her desk once or twice, but he didn't remember bossing her around. Just stealing kisses.

"You're sassy. Good thing you're sweet."

"So is that a yes to the help?" She was angling to move past the Employees Only sign, but he shook his head. His Santa-hatted staff had enough distractions. They didn't need Miranda in her pretty silk blouse smelling like flowers in their workspace. Or maybe that was just him. He'd never get the drinks out while they were still hot, and the guys would ride him hard for it.

"You sit. Relax." He slid a slice of apple pie Miranda's way, and her shoulders dropped a notch. "Want it à la mode?"

She shook her head, already lifting her fork. "You're busy."

He grabbed a scoop, bent to grab the pint of vanilla ice cream kept in the freezer below the counter, dug out a spoonful, and dropped it on her dessert. Her eyes rolled heavenward in bliss as she took the first bite.

"You're the best. And so is your pie."

"Don't you forget it," he said, pleased.

Around her, the team was telling tales from the rink again, laughter and loud voices filling the café. In the corner, one of his regulars, Kirk, sat watching, a gingerbread man raised halfway to his lips, and apparently forgotten, as he took in the scene.

Dak sprinkled cinnamon sugar on top of foamed milk, then drizzled some maple syrup, the scent bringing him back to his childhood. He needed to visit his family soon. He hadn't seen them in months, and with Christmas barely over two weeks away, he felt a stab of homesickness.

Miranda was laughing, and Dak pulled himself out of his reverie, warmed by the sound of happiness coming from the woman he loved. "Y'all sure can tell some tall tales. Fishermen have nothing on your stories."

Maverick and Leo, who were sandwiching Miranda at the bar, nodded in agreement.

Landon, seated on the other side of Leo, explained seriously, "You gotta be able to tell a good story. It's an NHL requirement. All those players overlooked on our farm teams that ooze talent? It's because they can't weave a good hockey tale. Nobody wants them in the locker room."

Miranda, who'd just taken a bite of her pie, laughed again, covering her mouth.

It was nice to see her in her element. Her crazy plans might just be working out for her, and last week's doubts had simply been the darkness before the dawn.

"How about the time the team emptied *my* mini bar, and I had to pay for it all?" Maverick complained good-naturedly. "Eight dollars for a bottle of water, Landon. The team doesn't cover incidentals."

"Sorry?" Landon looked up from his phone, dazed.

They all cracked up. "That's what you get when you're captain," someone called out. "You gotta guide us through the good times and the bad."

"And the dehydration!" Leo said.

Dak finished pouring several coffees, and Miranda, her pie done, jumped up to collect the full cups. "Let me help!"

"Sit, Miranda," he said gently.

"No, this is something I can do." She smiled, already turning to the room with the beverages. "Who ordered black coffee? It's hot, it's fresh, and it smells like nutmeg!"

A table near the door waved to her.

"Alright then. Suit yourself," Dak muttered as she headed

off, her hips swaying, her smile wide. She was beautiful, and he was a lucky man.

"Dakarai Morisette?" chirped a singsong, flirty voice.

It took Dak a moment to realize someone was looking for his attention.

"Quacky Dakky, is that you?" called the woman.

Dak cringed. The last time he'd heard that voice was in divorce court.

CHILLS RACED down Miranda's spine, and a burning heat replaced it. Jealousy. Red-hot jealousy.

She inhaled slowly, trying to cool herself down. Dak was a good-looking man, and he was allowed to know women. Pretty women. Pretty, skinny babes who used flirty, knowing tones with him. A tone Miranda felt should be reserved for the bedroom.

Miranda inhaled again, reminding herself that Dak wasn't the type to toss her aside because a woman with amazing legs waltzed in.

And couldn't this interloper see he was struggling to keep up with orders? Now wasn't the time.

"You forgot what I look like already?" Dak said, not looking up from the drink he was pouring. "That's more heartwarming than anyone could ever guess."

Miranda noted that quite a few men were eyeing the new arrival. Maverick, however, was securely focused on his beverage, as though afraid to be seen.

The woman had taken Miranda's stool, and Miranda came up behind her, saying firmly, but politely, "Excuse me. I was sitting there." She gave the woman a syrupy smile when she slowly looked over her shoulder.

The woman's gaze was long and held a hint of disdain as though Miranda was out of place. Yup. This gal was a queen bee. The kind who took perverse pleasure in bringing other women down, making them feel insignificant, and giving them new insecurities to keep them up at night.

"I'm so sorry," the woman purred in a fake polite voice. "I thought you were one of the staff."

Landon gave a bark of laughter. "Dressed like that?" He laughed until the woman's face turned red and she jerked her body off the stool in an insulted rage.

"What can I get for you, Jari?" Dak asked the woman as she wedged her way between Landon and Leo to stand at the bar. She eyed the long line of athletic men in jerseys. Then she aimed her enormous eyes toward Dak, her small chin pointing down as she gazed up—adoringly, of course—her slow eyelash batting worthy of a Disney cartoon heroine. Miranda was fairly certain she was going to barf.

"You know what I'd like," the woman purred.

Landon laughed into his drink, then shifted his shoulder to her, trying to mask his mirth.

Dak poured a cup of black coffee and put it down none too gently in front of her.

"It's only half full?" she whined, looking into the cup.

"Just like your perspective on life," Dak quipped, turning to help others.

Now it was Miranda's turn to suppress her amusement. Whoever this woman was, she was not welcome.

"I heard you're back with the NHL?" Jari asked, leaning forward. "Whatever happened to never-ever?"

Dak shot her a quick look.

"What? I'm allowed to read magazine articles about you. So, Mr. Never-Ever? Why?"

Dak's gaze hit Miranda's, and a slow-burning heat entered his dark eyes as the corner of his lips lifted. Miranda felt the tightness that had built in her chest ease and swirl away, her growing insecurities dissolving with them. "No reason."

"How's Amara?" Jari asked, watching Miranda and Dak, her eyes narrowing. Miranda could practically see her shift into competition mode.

"Fine," Dak replied, working on his next order.

"Eddie?"

"Good."

"Did he retire?"

"Did you want to order? We're busy."

"How are Nia and Omari? Is he taller than you? He must be. I haven't seen him in ages."

Miranda had no idea who this woman was talking about. Pets? Family? Friends? She obviously knew Dak, and knew him in a way she didn't. Was she the ex-wife?

"Did you need anything else, or did you just want to come in here to see if you still had a chance? Because the long answer is no."

"What's the short answer?" she asked, unaffected.

"Still no."

"Technically, that's a longer answer."

Dak continued serving up slices of pie, muffins, and other snacks to feed his friends, ignoring Jari.

"Fine. I'd like something," Jari said as Dak placed a slice of pie in front of Landon. "I'll have what he's having." She winked at Landon.

The man gave Dak an alarmed look, snagged his dessert, and slipped off his stool, abandoning it. Jari slithered onto it.

"You know," Miranda said mildly to the woman who was

now seated beside her, "these men have hopes and dreams. They're not just pieces of meat."

"I'll volunteer to be a piece of meat," called a rookie from the end of the bar, waving an arm to be seen around the bulk of muscle blocking Jari's view of him. Miranda wanted to sic a Dragons life coach on him to explain why women like Jari were bad news.

Come to think of it, maybe she really was Dak's ex-wife, and she was the reason Dak so heartily supported Miranda's interference into her players' lives.

Jari ignored the rookie's offer, focusing on Miranda. "I know who you are."

"Really?" Miranda said, in a flare of pettiness. "Because I have no clue who you are or why you're harassing my team."

The woman smirked, aware she'd gotten under Miranda's skin.

"I bet you know everything about these men," Jari said, running her eyes down Dak. "In Daki's best season, he scored eighty-five goals." She giggled. "And not all of them were on the ice."

"That's enough," Dak said harshly.

"Oh, you didn't tell her about me?" She turned her attention back to Miranda. "He did well on the ice, too. Got a nice little bonus. Well, the NHL isn't allowed to give bonuses anymore, but you know how things go. I'm sure you do the same for your best players. Bend a few rules. Play favorites. Hand out a few perks." Her tone took on a hint of suggestion.

"Jari, I said that's enough."

"She should know what she's getting into, that's all."

"I know what I signed up for," Miranda said, staring her down. "And I love every bit of it." Jari finally turned away, laughing, too loud and high to be real.

"Did you know he could have gone back to playing after his surgery?" Jari said over the rim of her cup, and to nobody in particular, but obviously for Miranda's sake. "He didn't have to retire."

Miranda forced herself not to look at Dak to confirm Jari's words. She could feel Jari eyeing her toned-down version of her Slays All Day outfit.

"Dak hates tuxedos so much he barely even went to his own award ceremonies. He had to have a few drinks first, didn't you, hon?"

Miranda looked to Dak this time, panic swelling in her mind that even though she understood Dak, maybe she didn't actually *know* him.

His expression was like a rock wall, his wide forearms crossed over his chest.

Maverick appeared beside Jari. "Maybe it would be a good time for you to go."

"He outright refused to come with me when I was awarded the Legal Eagle Upcoming Women's Award because he had to wear a tux."

"Can't take the man off Sugar Maple Farms, eh?" Landon asked.

"Like you're one to talk, you crazy Canuck," Dak quipped to Landon, never breaking his staring contest with Jari.

Jari turned to Miranda. "Have you ever won anything?"

"Yeah, we're going to win the Stanley Cup. Heard of it?"

The men roared and cheered. They began chanting, "The cup! The cup!"

Dak chuckled, and his shoulders relaxed.

Jari pushed off her stool. "I have to scoot. So lovely to run into you, Dak. I'll see you tomorrow."

"Not likely," Dak grumbled.

Jari blew a kiss and waved to the men, giggling as she left.

Miranda watched Dak. He knew next Friday's gala was black tie, and he'd RSVPed as her plus-one. What did that mean? That Jari was full of it, or that Dak was going to bail out?

And could he really still be on the ice as a player? What was the full story there?

And who were all those people Jari had mentioned?

If she truly loved Dak, shouldn't she at least know the names of his parents, family, and friends and know more about the injury that had removed him from his dream career?

She didn't know who Jari was to Dak exactly, but the woman had done what she'd come for. She'd made Miranda feel as though she might be the flavor of the week dazzled by all that was Dak rather than being his soulmate.

CHAPTER 9

$\mathcal{D}$ak burst out of the arena, Miranda in tow. He wanted to shout and celebrate, dance, lift Miranda and kiss her like the earth had just been saved from an alien attack.

"I can't believe they won," Miranda said, her cheeks flushed with joy. She looked stunned, happy.

"I really want to kiss you," he murmured, subtly giving her hand a quick squeeze.

"So do I." She gave him such a look of longing it was all he could do to resist pulling her into his arms right outside the arena's private entrance. The limo drivers lined up in the enclosed area wouldn't mind, would they? They'd be discreet if they saw a kiss or three.

"I'm struggling with keeping our relationship under wraps," he admitted. "So I've decided to resign so I can kiss you whenever I want, and especially after we win. Kisses anywhere, anytime."

"Don't you dare. You know how much I need you."

"Yeah?" He came closer, taunting her. "How much?"

"More than you'd ever believe."

"That's quite a bit." He fingered the hem of her jersey. She was wearing one of the team's hats with a pair of jeans and looked like a sexy, curvy puck bunny. He'd loved how into the game she'd been, cheering for her team from her exclusive private box seats. It made him wish he was still on the ice, his last name on the back of her jersey.

He snuck a kiss, but to his surprise, she deepened it, twining her arms around his shoulders. When they broke apart, he whispered, "What does that mean?"

"I'm happy and I momentarily gave in." She didn't budge but remained in his arms, and he tightened his grip, going in for another delicious kiss.

The door behind them opened and closed, and Miranda slipped from his embrace, murmuring, "I hate this."

They nodded to the group of suited men who eyed Miranda's figure on their way by. Dak wanted to take her hand and show them that under no circumstances were they to give her lingering looks.

But no. He had to be a respectful colleague. No more shared looks that lasted a little too long, or voices that softened when they spoke to each other, or heads that met too closely as they swapped secrets.

"Is it really a big deal if the press finds out we're dating?" he asked.

She took him in, her dark eyes dancing over him. "You really want to try?"

He nodded.

He could see she was tempted. She wanted it, too. But she shook her head, blinking away whatever thoughts had been sending her leaning his way. "It's going to be a lot. Too much."

"But what if it isn't? Your players are hooking up faster than spaghetti and cheese. That might distract the press."

"Spaghetti and cheese?"

"I couldn't think of anything else."

She moved toward the limos, slowly, her bottom lip between her teeth as she considered his request to go public.

"I already told you I can handle publicity," he said.

"I know."

"And with Christmas in two weeks, we're both extra busy. We hardly see each other, and when we do, we have to pretend we don't care about each other. It's messing with my mind."

"Mine, too."

"Anyway, half the team already assumes we're together."

"What?" she squeaked.

"Well…" He chuckled. "You and my ex were practically fighting over me at the Gingerbread, you know. Most bosses don't get jealous of ex-wives like that."

"We weren't fighting! And I can't believe you married *her*." Miranda gave a harrumph, and crossed her arms.

He laughed as she blushed.

The arena doors opened again, and the family that had been in the Dragons' Special Guests Box set up near center ice came outside. The Samson family was decked out in their free Dragons merchandise, and they were smiling. Looking at them, it was hard to believe they had a chronically ill child.

"You were a good luck charm, Cherice," Miranda announced, moving toward the little girl in the wheelchair. "Our first win of the month, and our second of the season. How were your seats?"

"We loved being so close to the ice! Thank you," said Mrs. Samson as her daughter grinned.

Miranda and Dak fussed over Cherice and admired her signed-by-Maverick, game-winning puck. He's scored the winning goal against Lafayette, and Dak loved the justice that had allowed his pal to win against the team that had discarded him.

Cherice nodded, hugging the puck to her chest like the prized possession it was. "When I'm better, I'm going to play defense like Maverick Blades!"

The Samsons thanked Miranda and Dak for the amazing evening, and Dak helped them get settled into the Dragons-sponsored limo, folding up Cherice's wheelchair for the driver to put in the trunk.

Miranda was smiling when he turned after waving to the departing car. "That was a special night, Miranda." He'd coordinated a few things, but the idea had been all hers.

"Every home game," she chirped happily.

He slipped his arm around her shoulders and she quieted, her energy radiating happiness.

"Your grandfather would be proud."

She grinned. "Right?"

And, not caring if anyone saw, he kissed her again.

MIRANDA DID her best to politely shoulder her way through the cluster of reporters surrounding the front doors of the Dragons' head office. Reporters shouted questions and cameras and microphones were thrust at her. She couldn't make out a single word anyone was saying.

The security guards rushed from the building, creating space for her to get to the doors. She gave them a grateful thanks and escaped into the large lobby, which was decorated for Christmas.

"I already told them there would be a press conference this afternoon," Daisy-Mae said, meeting her by the elevator in a festive, fuzzy red sweater. "But they refused to leave."

"Where are the twins?" Miranda asked. Mark and Nuvella were in charge of publicity, and they should be down here dealing with this. Daisy-Mae was in charge of merchandising and ticket-holder experiences, along with her role as the mascot handler. Why was she paying Mark and Nuvella if Daisy-Mae seemed to be doing their job every time she turned around?

"They were in a meeting about the gala."

Miranda groaned involuntarily. The gala. She still had a list of things to take care of for next week's event, *and* she still needed a dress. Talk about an opportunity for torture. Not just all the fake smiling and contortions she'd have to go through so people would open their wallets, but the dress. She knew how she wanted to look, but designers seemed bent on minimizing and masking her curves with excessive fabric rather than letting them ride.

"They're on the phones now—they were ringing off the hook," Daisy-Mae explained as they moved past the lobby's giant Christmas tree. "I said I'd come down here. I hope that's okay?"

"Yes, of course. Thank you." Miranda stepped into the elevator with Daisy-Mae, letting out a long exhale when the doors finally closed. "That was intense. Who knew winning a game would cause such a fuss?"

Daisy-Mae stared at her as though she couldn't decide what to say, which was very unlike her.

"What? What happened?" Miranda asked, panic setting in.

"Nobody has shown you...?" Daisy-Mae frowned and

whipped her phone from the cute bag slung across her torso. She turned the screen to Miranda.

"Oh," Miranda said, the air rushing from her lungs.

Daisy-Mae gave her a look of sympathy, then grinned. "He's worth making a fuss over. And it's a great photo."

"And this will probably ruin everything between us." Miranda moaned, catching sight of the less-than-flattering headline about her dating the former NHL party boy—her boy toy—and how she'd put him in charge of helping sick children.

She wasn't sure it could get much worse than that for publicity.

The elevator doors opened on the top floor, and she tucked away her personal pity party. Business time.

People from her team were already waiting outside her office, including the PR twins and the GM. Great. It really was *that* bad.

Jeremy, her assistant, was racing around, offering cups of hot cocoa, while wearing a pair of reindeer antlers. It was then that she realized Christmas had thrown up all over the waiting area. Several Christmas trees of various sizes, fake gifts, lights, and even fake snow on the windowsills.

She still needed to do her Christmas shopping. Was she supposed to get something for Dak? They'd been dating for such a short time, and these headlines were sure to put an end to things. Maybe it was good she was behind on preparing for the holidays. She didn't have to return his gift if she didn't have one.

"I'm sure it will all work out," Daisy-Mae said sympathetically before the elevator doors closed, taking her to the fourth floor to continue her work on Miranda's personal mess.

"I'll need a minute," Miranda announced to her staff as everyone began jostling and speaking at once.

Miranda closed her office door behind her and leaned against it, allowing herself a moment of regret. Dak was the best, and she may have just had the most amazing—and shortest—relationship of her entire life so far.

Why had she given in? She knew this could happen.

With a sigh, she headed to her desk, knowing Jeremy would have sent all of the pertinent headlines to her tablet for her to look through as per their usual morning routine.

Miranda stared at the screen, frantically flipping through the articles. There were quite a few about the team's win, only one or two mentioning the new charity, as it had already been amply covered on Wednesday, but the vast majority of them featured her and Dak kissing outside the arena.

She let her tablet clatter onto her desktop as she leaned back, eyes closed. What was she going to do? She slumped forward, letting her cheek rest on the desk's cool surface.

The papers, unlike her, had recognized Dak. They wasted no time digging up the worst of his past and were now questioning her for putting this former rookie party boy in charge of an important part of the team's charity. Boy toy. The term was so degrading! They even accused her of using her power as his employer to get what she wanted from him.

She picked up her tablet, looking at the photos again, thinking maybe her perspective had been skewed by her panic and shock.

No. They were that bad.

The kiss they'd captured couldn't be played off as anything other than what it was. Hot.

Her team had earned an important win this week, and she wanted it touted, not overshadowed by a kiss.

It had been the Dragons' first game since their work at the hospital, since having a family in the Dragons' Special Guest Box at center ice.

Coincidence?

She didn't think so. The team had come together, and that had played a bigger role than Lafayette's lack of leadership. Her team was doing good things and the win was *theirs*.

And she was going to make sure the media let them claim it.

Miranda braced herself and let her staff into her office. Time to begin the damage control. Too bad there wasn't some for her heart.

DAK STRODE into Miranda's office, knowing she would be freaking out and ready to shield him by ending their relationship.

He came around her desk, leaning down to kiss her softly. "How are you doing?"

"Did you see the headlines?"

He could feel her withdrawing, pulling back.

"I did."

"So, there's only one thing to do," Miranda said as he took the floral chair across from her desk. She had her hair up in a twist at the nape of her neck, slim chains of white gold dangling from her perfect earlobes. She looked gorgeous and in control. Sexy beyond belief.

But he wasn't excited about the way she was staying behind the mammoth piece of furniture.

"Yes. Date publicly. Finally." He leaned back, crossing his ankles out in front of him.

"Dak, I'm sorry," she said, not looking at him, "but I can't afford to have my personal life impact you, the charity, your career and reputation, or even the team. It's not fair to the families that are trusting us to take good care of their children. I can't let this negative attention shine on them as well."

She had a point, but using the families felt like a low blow.

"How is who you're dating any of their business?" he asked angrily, pointing to the wall as if it represented the press. He wanted to punch something. He loved hockey, but he hated the way the public got to determine someone's reputation. Look at Maverick. He'd protected a woman back in Lafayette, and now everyone thought he snuck around with married women.

At his sharp tone, Miranda had blinked and leaned back.

He knew his job was to roll over and give up, allow her to deliver her breakup speech and let the press win.

There was no way.

"Dak," Miranda said gently, "they're bringing up things from your past."

"I've moved beyond all of that."

"What about your family?"

"They know what I was like, and they know I've changed. Everyone who matters to me knows."

Miranda was shaking her head, not accepting his words.

"Your publicity team told you to break things off, didn't they?" He leaned forward, realizing he'd stumbled on the truth by the way her mouth tightened, the pain in her beautiful stormy dark eyes. "How do they get to tell you how to run your life, but I don't?"

"Dak…" Her tone held a warning. "I'm trying to protect you."

"This can be used as a stepping-stone. Negative publicity can easily be turned into good."

"The team disagrees. It could go sideways, and I can't do that to the players. They're already dealing with a lot of crap because of me."

"So you won't allow yourself a life because the press is gunning for you? Because they finally found something that will shut you up, make you hide away and behave the way a good woman should?"

Miranda gasped. She stood, rage filling her eyes.

He stood as well, softening his tone. "You're going to deny me, and what we have between us? For who? For what purpose? They'll never let you be, no matter who you're with."

She wouldn't look at him.

"If you run, if you give in…it'll only make it worse. They'll never rest."

"I just want what's best for you." To his surprise, her eyes were filled with tears when she finally looked up at him. "I don't want to hurt you."

He moved around the desk, leaning against it so he could slip between her and the beastly office piece. "Miranda," he whispered, gently touching her chin. "Keep dating me. I'll always have your back. We can be strong and united against these jerks. Giving up will hurt me more than anything they could ever print. Let me try and fix this for us."

She gave him a pleading look.

"Come on, Peanuts."

"Peanuts?" she asked, her voice small, her eyes damp.

"Yeah, Peanuts. Where's your competitive side? The woman who beat my shelling record? You gonna let these losers win and turn you into someone you're not?"

A tear fell, and Dak realized with a heavy blow how much she cared for him. It was outweighing her need to defeat the reporters and naysayers. She wanted to protect him more than win. It floored him, hollowed his gut.

"Please," he begged. "Let me try." He caressed her cheek, and she pressed it to his hand. The hope in her expression made him surge on. "I know how to talk to the press, and I've been in a delicate personal position before. When my marriage failed shortly after it started, guess who was there? And look! I survived."

He gave her a wry smile even though thinking about the past hurt. But letting the press dig into his life again? Not a chance. He was ready for Round Two. Especially since he had something—someone—worth fighting for.

"You and I are doing something positive—not trying to murder each other like my ex and I were." He winked, and she gave him a feeble, uncertain smile. "You and I are not backing down. We've done nothing wrong."

He added, "Remember the way Cherice was beaming after the game. That's what matters. Don't let some headlines ruin those moments."

"But that's what I'm trying to protect," she protested.

"I know, and I want to help. If you push me away now, the reporters will be making up stuff about your love life from now until the end of time. Breakups. Baby bumps. Rehab. Despair over me dating someone else."

"You wouldn't dare!"

He almost laughed at the flash in her eyes.

He pulled her into his arms. With a shudder she held onto him, and they stayed quiet for a long moment, then Miranda leaned back, watching him, her fiery resolve returning.

"If things aren't better in a few days, we need to reassess our relationship," she warned.

He smiled, his worries easing, his heart soaring. "Woman, Rome wasn't built in a day. Give me at least a week."

"Fine, but do we get to hide out at my ranch all weekend?"

"We're going to be breaking out the champagne by then," he said confidently.

"It's only Thursday!"

"*And* no matter what happens, I'm your plus-one next Friday."

Her relieved smile was all the reward and motivation he needed. He dusted his hands as though his job had already been completed. Now all he had to do was set things right for the woman he hoped would never try to release him again.

CHAPTER 10

Miranda had never dreaded being in front of the press so much as that afternoon. Thankfully, the general manager and coaches were staying on script, obeying the PR team's commands to not comment on Miranda's personal life or even the charity. They were only to answer questions about the team and last night's win and also mention the new policy that anyone viewing Dragons practices now had to stay in tier two or higher in the stands.

The rink had been flooded with women since the Dragons had spent time at the hospital, and they were proving to be a distraction.

Miranda had informed her PR team that she and Dak weren't breaking up and were going to date publicly. They hadn't loved that.

In return, Dak was to stay silent about their relationship during his portion of the press conference—he could discuss the Dragons' Special Guest Box, the Samson family, the visit to the hospital earlier in the week, and that was all.

As well, Miranda was to stay off to the side and ignore

questions directed at her. They'd actually wanted her out of the room, but she'd insisted she be present. As Dak had stated, show no fear.

The coaches and the GM finished up, and Dak took to the small table, sitting in front of the Dragons logo. He was wearing a tailored charcoal suit, which Miranda guessed was likely from his NHL days as players wore suits to and from games. Due to his workouts and semi-recent retirement, the jacket still fit him perfectly. The man could be a fashion model and sell her a closet of menswear, he was so tasty.

He adjusted the microphone, hands already flying in the air as reporters spoke over each other, eager to take the first bite out of him and reminding her of a tank crowded with piranhas at feeding time.

Miranda felt like she'd sweat more in the last five minutes than in a week's worth of workouts.

If she actually kept any of the appointments with her trainer, that was. The man was a beast, intent on bringing her to the underworld as fast as possible.

If the next few moments went south, she wouldn't be able to do the date-in-public thing with Dak. There would be no bringing the sexiest man to the gala on her arm, or even the possibility of finally enjoying a gala.

"Before I take any of your questions," Dak said, "I'd like to introduce our special guests. The Samson family has graciously agreed to answer any questions you might have about their experience in the new Dragons' Special Guest Box, which our team owner, Miranda Fairchild, had set up at center ice." He went on to explain the details of the program, as well as how much the charity had already brought in to date.

Dak stood as Miranda ushered the Samson family into the

press room. She gave them a quick hug before they joined Dak on the platform for their introduction.

Miranda wanted to kiss Dak for how smooth and controlled he was. Talk about sexy. Smart, too. Bring in the team's feel-good story and prevent the sharks from doing any fatal damage. Some reporters looked conflicted, unsure whether they should be annoyed by the distraction or feel all warm and fuzzy.

The family took questions like a champ, and they were so positive Miranda feared it would sound as though they'd been given a script. Then again, the pure joy on Cherice's face said it all. The Dragons' Box experience was special, and anyone who didn't see that was either blind or part Grinch.

In fact, the press seemed to loathe giving the team publicity about the players literally carrying children out of the hospital as firetrucks arrived. It had commanded notice online, though. Social media had blown up with trending hashtags and women Photoshopping themselves into photos so they were in the arms of the NHL stars.

She caught Dak's eyes and smiled, feeling such deep gratitude for his role in the charity as well as his pep talk about ignoring the naysayers. They were doing a good thing, and the people who wanted her to fail could take a hike.

Miranda walked out with the family, laughing with the kids who were so excited they likely wouldn't sleep for days. She gave them hugs and goodbyes, handing them off to Daisy-Mae. Then Miranda returned to the press room where Dak was at the microphone again. Her stomach tightened, and the dread came back. Things could go so wrong, so quickly.

"I'll take two questions," Dak stated. "Then this press conference is over."

The room erupted with noise.

When Dak remained silent, the room quieted. Miranda feared the reporters would think she was muzzling him by restricting the number of questions.

"Wow," Dak said with an amused chuckle, "sounds like those were all personal questions rather than about the good work the Dragons' charity is doing for our community. I didn't know y'all loved me so much." He'd added a fake Texan drawl, which was charming, and her fears subsided. He knew what he was doing up there, and he'd make things better. Just like he promised.

"I'm not surprised, though, because who wants to report on something good when you have something juicy such as the team's owner having found herself a boyfriend." He let the gentle reprimand sink in, and Miranda dared a quick look at the gathered reporters to see how they were reacting. Mostly they seemed impatient.

"You know what's funny?" Dak asked. "I don't ever remember hearing anything about Larry Tanenbaum or Murray Edwards or any other team owner's personal life or who they were dating. Why is Miranda Fairchild so interesting? It's because of me, isn't it?" He gave them a big, toothy grin. It was cocky, charming, and a little bit sexy. Or maybe it was the way he was toying with them, scolding them, calling them on their double standards that had her wanting to run up there and kiss him.

As he answered the first question—a tough one—he remained the man she knew. There was no backtracking or excuses, no doublespeak or vague words that meant nothing. He was straight-up, honest and kind.

And most of all, he was standing up for her. Publicly.

She needed to marry this man and take him everywhere she went.

"Miranda and I are dating; I can confirm that."

Her head snapped up. That was on the No list from the twins.

"And we would greatly appreciate if you respected our privacy like you would any other team owner. In no way is our personal relationship going to impact what we do here on the team." He gave a big grin again. "Unless, of course, we're the team's lucky charm and are responsible for last night's win. In which case, if you want your city to have a winning team, you'd better keep us happy and very much in love."

HE SAID LOVE.

Miranda couldn't process anything else as Dak ended the press conference, walked to her side, took her hand, and led her out of the noisy room.

She felt giddy, like her head was filled with helium.

Dak drew her down the hallway as the room emptied behind them, the sound of hurrying footsteps coming their way.

"You realize it sounds like we're taking credit for the team's win?" Miranda said breathlessly.

"I didn't say I was perfect," Dak said with a grin.

"Well, I think you are. You were amazing in there. Did you arrange all of that?" She pointed toward the room behind them, glancing over her shoulder. A reporter was almost upon them, and Dak quickly pushed them through a door marked Private.

"I did," he said on the other side of the door. "But Daisy-Mae helped me."

"Why am I paying my PR team when I have the two of you?" she asked in wonder.

"Don't worry, they're still doing their job. You and I just kind of exploded their world. And then Daisy-Mae and I sort of railroaded them as well. They're good sports." There was that grin again. Intoxicating, confident, full of happiness. Because of her? It felt impossible that she could make this marvelous man this happy. That everything in her life might finally fall into perfect place.

"They must wonder why they took this job."

Dak laughed.

"I don't know how I got so lucky finding you."

He gave her a sweet kiss. "Just keep on believing it, honey."

"I don't have to. I'm living it."

"Speaking of living it, you know you have to go to all the games with me now?"

"Why's that?"

"We're the team's lucky charm. The cameras will need to see us there, kissing and being in love." His fingers were entwined with hers, his smile contagious. "I bet they give us a ship name."

"A what?" He'd said love again, and her mind had returned to spinning. "Oh, right. A cutesy relationship name."

As weird as it would feel, having all eyes on them as well as the speculation that would surely ensue, it felt special, romantic. As though she'd finally been chosen by someone so spectacular that others wanted to be a part of it.

Dak held her tighter. "I bet they choose Dakaranda."

"Meh."

"Morrisfair? Combine our last names?"

"More is fair? You're bad at this."

"You chose me."

"Are you actually my boyfriend now? Officially? In all capacities of the definition?"

"Yes, and we need a ship name because social media goes nuts for that sort of thing. Maybe the twins can plant it in the media for us."

"Doesn't the public create their own ship names?"

"Yeah, but you need to change your name to something better," he teased. "They're never going to come up with any good ones."

"I think you need to change your name!"

They had begun moving again, heading toward the exit. They were about to break out into the December chill when Miranda realized it was still the middle of the workday. She needed to turn around, go upstairs and work.

But this afternoon was worthy of celebration, wasn't it? And as the boss she could play hooky whenever she liked. And today she liked.

Dak pushed the door open, and they were blasted with sunshine. His car was parked a few spaces down, no reporters or cameramen in sight.

"So?" she asked.

"Dinner," Dak said firmly.

"It's only two in the afternoon!"

"It takes an hour to get to Sweetheart Creek, and that's where I'm taking you. We can enjoy the evening, hang out all day tomorrow, then show up at tomorrow night's home game and bring forth another victory. What do you say?"

"I can't believe you're already using our relationship to get out of work."

He laughed. "Okay, so we come back for work in the morning. Up for a private celebration with me? Mrs. Fisher at the Longhorn promised to have the chef make us onion ring burgers the next time we came in, as long as we don't play ring toss with the onion rings like last time."

The idea of escaping for the evening warmed her heart. They climbed into his car, but before he started the engine, she asked, "So back there…"

"When I said we're in love?"

"Yeah." She waited for his answer, unable to look at him, unable to bear it if he said he'd been playing to the audience, putting a positive spin on things for the sake of the team and the charity.

"What about it?"

"Are you?"

"In love with you?" Dak shifted in his seat when she darted a look his way. "What? You don't think it's possible?"

An NHL star in love with her? Well, yes, and no. But mostly no. She was chubby, and not the right type or shape. She wasn't from a sports family or even all that athletic. What if he enjoyed taking hiking vacations and she couldn't keep up? She didn't even know how to skate or play hockey.

"I think…"

"No, no thinking. Feel. Do you feel it? This energy between us? The way we instantly connected?"

She faced him in the seat. She felt shy, nervous. Like she was thirteen and had her first real crush. He was so handsome, strong, kind. Everything.

He was everything she wanted, and she was so afraid to have him, already fearing she'd lose him.

"Miranda?" he asked, catching her attention. "You know I'm falling in love with you even though it feels crazy fast."

She inhaled, letting the miracle of his words warm her soul. A grin was forming, and she was powerless against it. She wanted to squeal, to call her friends and breathlessly announce that Dak—Dakarai Morisette—a retired NHL star, was in love with her!

"You like that?" he teased.

She nodded, still smiling, unable to speak.

"And are you going to make me smile like that too?" he asked.

She shifted fully, so she was facing him as much as she could in the bucket seat. "Dak, you are the best darn thing that's marched into my life. Maybe ever."

"Maybe?" He quirked a brow.

"Don't get cocky. It's still early days."

He threw back his head of dark hair as though she was killing him and gripped the steering wheel. "Early days?"

"But yeah. You're my boyfriend. My gala date." Her voice grew quiet. "And yes, I'm falling in love with you, too."

She leaned across the space between them, kissing him, sealing in their love.

In the Longhorn, their meals completed, Dak sat back, taking in Miranda. His gaze kept straying to her lips. He wanted to scoot out of here, find somewhere private, and kiss his girlfriend.

The woman who was falling for him. He was moving fast, like always, but this time it felt different. It felt *right*.

Mrs. Fisher, the waitress with the teased hair and wrinkled face, collected their plates. "How was it, hon?"

"Very good. Thank you. It was difficult not playing ring toss, though."

"A promise is a promise," she teased, giving them a wink.

She left to take their plates to the kitchen, and a new country and western song about Christmas started up. Dak hadn't realized there were so many Christmas songs about cowboys.

He caught Miranda's attention. "I'm looking forward to going to more games with you." He leaned forward, giving her that kiss even though the diner was filling up with supper traffic. He could get used to this.

Wednesday night's game had been fun, and not just because they won. He'd enjoyed watching Miranda get into the game, her enthusiasm contagious as she'd cheered and stood when her team made a goal. And for all her competitiveness, she was a good sport, acknowledging excellent plays made by the other team, clapping when they scored as well. Even though, personally, he wanted complete shutouts.

"I like being broadcast on the Jumbotron," she said, giggling. The cameras had been on her frequently throughout the game, putting her image on the big screen.

"You're an attention hog. I hadn't expected that."

"I rarely see the other team owners up on that screen."

"So, this is a competition?"

She shrugged, demure and playful.

He laughed. He loved this woman.

"So tomorrow's home game?" he asked.

"I'll be there, and you're welcome to sit with me."

"Dakaranda will be in the house! The Dragons' lucky charm!"

She smiled, then grew quiet. "So Jari? She lives nearby?" Her joy had been replaced by hesitance.

"My ex lives in Houston."

Three hours away. Sometimes he wished for more distance, but typically she stayed out of his life so it all worked out okay. Typically.

"Didn't you cyberstalk me before we started dating?" he teased Miranda. "Do you even know who I am?"

"Well, apparently you scored a lot of *goals*," she teased right back, arms crossed.

"Not funny." Not at all.

"So jokes about your ex are off limits? I'll make a note."

"Jari and I had hopes that didn't pan out. We didn't know each other at the level we should have. She wanted the fame and glory, and I thought I did too. I wanted to do real life, and she said that would be great, but we never saw it. Not together. Our visions of fame and real life were pretty different in the end. It made it difficult to live together."

"Could you have gone back to the NHL after your shoulder injury?"

Absently, he rolled his shoulder. "Yes," he said carefully. He wasn't sure Miranda's competitive side would understand his decision. In his mind, the choice had been clear. To everyone else, he knew it hadn't been.

"I hear a 'but'?" she asked gently.

"My shoulder isn't the same. It isn't as strong or as powerful. There's a chance that winding up for a slapshot, I could re-injure it again. The second time you hurt a joint after surgery, you might not get as lucky with the recovery." He pulled in a deep breath, choosing his words carefully, hoping she'd understand. "I realized I could either go out on top of my game, or I could return and hobble along until I was forced out. But if I chose to play at that high level again, I'd be in semi-constant pain and my shoulder would need constant therapy. I'd worry. I'd fear every ache was something worse than it was. I'd always be holding back so I wouldn't have a momentary lapse and completely debilitate myself permanently."

She nodded. "It must have been a hard decision."

"I keep telling myself hockey isn't everything." Dak pushed

his hands into his thick hair, recalling the internal battle he'd struggled through for months after deciding. Having the café to pour himself into had helped, but the doubts and anger still surfaced. Even now.

"Yeah," she said softly.

He wanted to believe that this player-centric owner understood his decision and that this understanding was at the core of why he was so attracted to her.

She was looking at him, chest expanded like she wanted to say something.

"Anything you wanna know, you can just ask," he said.

She exhaled. "I know. And same goes for me."

He gave her a dry smile. "Any ex-husbands in your past?"

She laughed so suddenly she choked. She shook her head, amused. "No. Definitely not. Not even close." Her expression closed up, sealing over pain.

"Well," he said, holding her gaze, connecting with her, "hopefully you'll only ever need one."

Her lips parted, her eyes dancing. Then the intent of his words sunk in and he saw a flicker of fear dart across her expression.

What if he was genuinely offering marriage—and was he? He might be. He'd considered the idea several times already.

But if he was, there was a risk he was jumping in too fast all over again because he thought he'd found someone who understood him. Either way, he noted her fear, which meant Miranda Fairchild wasn't as ready as he was.

CHAPTER 11

The café was a zoo, just like Dak's manager had said. Ever since he and Miranda went public, followed by the Dragons getting some good publicity, the Gingerbread Café had been swamped with dolled-up, beautiful women. He'd had to hire more staff and institute a pay-to-stay policy so the gawkers didn't prevent the real customers from coming in, scared and wide-eyed.

Maybe he should have just gone with it, charged men an entry fee and renamed the place The Dating Zone and made better profits.

Being too busy wasn't a bad problem to have, except Dak needed to be somewhere, not here dealing with the crisis of having more customers than his staff could handle.

And that place he needed to be was the gala. Over an hour ago.

Thankfully, Miranda had insisted on them taking separate cars, so at least she wasn't still at home wondering if her date had abandoned her.

"I'll do one more thing and then I'm gone," he warned his

manager as he passed her with a tray of clean cups. She gave him a harried nod.

He hadn't even texted Miranda. He'd put his phone in his car's console to charge when he arrived two hours ago, naively believing that if he left his phone, it would pressure him to *not* be late, because he wouldn't be able to shoot Miranda a text. Boy, that had been some faulty logic, and now he was a jerk.

He hurried back to the front, hit by the wall of strong coffee and the increasing volume as warm bodies filled his café. He was failing. He was letting customers down. He was letting Miranda down. No matter what he did, he wasn't winning today.

He slipped behind the counter, untying the apron he'd tossed over his tux, intent on getting out of the café before his girlfriend believed he'd forgotten about her.

"I would've come here sooner if I'd known there was a handsome young man wearing a tuxedo who'd take my order," said a familiar voice.

Dak's thoughts and worries fell to the wayside as he placed the voice.

His mom was here.

Not in Quebec. Not thousands of miles away. But right here.

He came around the counter, and his mom put out her arms, all smiles. "Surprise!"

"Business must be good," his father said, standing behind her.

"What are you doing here?" Dak asked, wrapping his mom in an embrace before shaking hands with his dad.

"We thought we'd come down for a little surprise," Amara

said. "You said you've been busy, so we're here to help. And to spend Christmas with you."

"With me?"

"Yes. You won't have to race off to the airport to go play in a game for the first time in your adult life, so we thought we'd descend on you. I hope you don't mind."

"Not at all, but what about Nia and Oh-no?" His siblings had spent a lot of their lives bending their worlds and schedules to fit his.

His mom laughed. "Don't you dare let Omari hear you call him that."

Dak smirked. The old nickname was a surefire way to get under his brother's skin. Dak would be calling his brother Oh-no at least once over Christmas. Guaranteed. And he was pretty sure his brother would return the favor with some of his own tried and true methods of annoyance.

"They're excited to come to Texas and skip the snowy weather for a week! They arrive in a few days and we have a lovely hotel booked, so we won't be in your way."

"Nonsense. Stay with me. You can't stay in a hotel over Christmas."

"We'll sort all of that out later. It looks like you're off somewhere?" His dad suggested, taking in Dak's tux.

"You look so handsome." With a proud smile, his mom ran her hands down the sleeves of his tuxedo jacket. She had streaks of gray in her curly black hair now, but her skin still had that miraculous youthful glow where she could be thirty, but certainly not sixty, her actual age. His father, however, looked like the older scallywag he'd always been.

"I'm supposed to be on my way to a gala."

"Oh! For the charity. I remember you mentioning that."

"Because you teased me mercilessly about having to wear a tux?"

His mom giggled, her eyes dancing. "You've always been so funny about bow ties. This must be a very important night." She reached out to straighten his with a clucking sound. "It looks like you've strangled this thing."

"It's the other way around, I think."

"You look *so* handsome." She beamed at him, stepping back. "My goodness, we have poor timing, though."

"Not at all."

She gave him one of those patented mother looks that suggested she wasn't buying his attempt to make her feel better.

"Mom, truly. I'm happy you're here."

A woman with a messy bun stood at the maple counter, tapping her fingers impatiently while loudly clearing her throat.

"Sorry, I've got to take care of this order. I'll be right back."

"What can we do to help?" his father called, his parents tailing him into the Employees Only zone behind the counter.

"Can you make a caramel macchiato?" Dak asked with a grin.

His dad, in his deep tenor, said, "Son, I can take out the trash."

"We'll clear some tables for you," his mom said. She turned to her husband. "You find a rag and wipe down the tables after I clear them. We'll worry about trash cans when they're about to overflow. We need to triage, baby. The place is coming apart at the seams."

Dak gave them a grateful smile and took the woman's order. "Clean rags are in the cabinet underneath," he told his mom, gesturing in the right direction as the woman swiped her card. "Spray bottles are for the tables."

He really needed to hire even more staff. It was uncool to have his vacationing, retired parents working in his café because he wasn't taking care of his own business. Even though they were happy to do it, they'd put in their time. Not just with driving him to every hockey practice, game, and tournament, but arranging family vacations around his hockey camps and the juniors. They'd already bent so much of their lives around him.

And yeah, they'd say it was their job as parents and they loved doing it, but at some point, he really needed to share them with his siblings and quit working them all the time.

"I've got to go," he said to his manager after he slid a mocha to the woman in the messy bun. There was still a lineup, staff scrambling instead of working systematically as a team like he'd trained them to. But at some point the team had to learn to swim through it all without him.

Dak removed his green apron, catching sight of his mom fussing over a customer, his dad wiping down tables. He couldn't leave his parents here to work.

And his new manager was floundering on the increased pressure today. What kind of business owner would he be if he didn't support his staff?

But he couldn't stand up his girlfriend. Not at a charity event where he was playing a pretty important role.

He closed his eyes and dropped his apron into the laundry bin in the back room.

Think, Dak, think.

Who could he call in to help out for a few hours?

What was he thinking? It would take them at least a half hour to arrive, making him over two hours late for the gala.

Unforgivable.

Or he could just close the doors and tell everybody to get the heck out because he had a date. He grinned, opening his eyes.

"Who're you thinking of? Not one of those beautiful women out front? They sure grow them gorgeous in Texas," his mom said, setting down a bin of dirty dishes. "Must be someone special?"

"She is, and I'm currently standing her up."

"Oh, my." Her expression turned to concern. She began pushing on his back, directing him toward the exit. "We'll figure things out here. If you have a woman wearing the equivalent of a tuxedo somewhere in this city, you need to be there. *Now*." She gave him a stern look that reminded him of his youth. That expression meant business. Reflexively, he shut his mouth, looked around for a minivan to jump into with his hockey bag in hand.

"If it gets too overwhelming, just tell everyone to leave and then lock the doors behind them," he said. "I won't mind."

"You know we would never do that."

"It's an actual option, Mom. You're retired and on vacation."

"And bored. We came down here specifically to help." She grabbed a nearby tea towel and snapped it at him. "Get marching, Buster."

Overcome with gratitude, he bent, giving her a quick peck on the cheek. "You're the best, Mom."

"I plan on meeting this woman."

"So Dad can throw her on the barbecue and grill her like a steak?" He gave his mom a frown. "No, thanks."

"You mean to say that you're dating a woman who can't

handle your father? How's that working out seeing as you're as tough as he is, just in a different way?"

"Okay, okay," Dak said, relenting. "The two of you can meet her." If he didn't let them meet Miranda on his own terms, they'd ambush her. It seemed as though Jari had made them a bit protective. And honestly, he wouldn't mind the sound check. Just to be sure Miranda really was the woman he was meant to be with, and he wasn't rushing things like he feared.

"Tomorrow," his mom said firmly.

Tomorrow was Saturday. Away games for the team. Getaway weekend to Miranda's. Her home in the country had already become a routine, an escape, something to look forward to. But harder to get to due to their mutual busyness. It felt like real life was constantly offside and cherry picking his timetable while the referee was suffering zero-zero vision.

Dak needed more time. *They* needed more time. Because he was falling hard and fast, and he needed to make sure Miranda had the time to keep up.

"WHERE IS DAKARAI? I'm eager to meet him," Miranda's mother said, eyeing Miranda's red velvet dress. "I wish you would have let me pick your gown and that you'd have taken my advice with your hair. Having it down slims the face. A few curls and a pretty clip and your hair would look very fetching and not at all too informal, like you argued."

"I like my dress." Miranda ran her hands over the soft fabric. It was soothing, comfortable, and enunciated her curves. She also didn't mind the way it made her mother's neck grow a little longer and her nostrils flare with displeasure.

Plus, this stunning red looked amazing with her dark hair and olive skin. She didn't need Dak here to tell her as much, because she knew. Maybe she wasn't hot in the standard everyone-is-the-same kind of way, but a new hot. One she could rock.

"Well? Where is he?" insisted her mother. "I'm starting to think all that kissing for the camera at the games is just for show."

"I'm sure he just got held up at the café and will be here soon," Miranda said mildly, refusing to let her mom increase the niggling self-doubts that were already crowding her. More squeezed in with each fifteen minutes that passed and every time someone new asked where the absent man was.

The past few weeks had been busy for both of them, with everything taking off all at once. The Dragons' winning streak, the charity, publicity, his café, their images on the Jumbotron at every home game as they were now officially dubbed the team's lucky charm. It was great, but they needed some time alone together. Then again, she wanted to be with him every hour of the day and missed him as soon as he was gone. There might not be enough one-on-one time to satisfy her at the moment.

"I thought he worked for you?" her mother was saying. "Shouldn't you command him to be on time? He's not making a wonderful impression."

"He works with the charity, yes, but he also owns a café. I'm sure he'll be here shortly. The café has been very busy, as has the charity. We've had an incredible amount of new supporters these past two weeks."

"I thought he was giving a speech." Her mother produced a program and waved it.

"He'll be here," Miranda said, struggling to maintain her smile.

"Well, I don't know what's going on with the two of you, but I think you need to keep your options open. You're not getting any younger, and it's smart for a woman to have choices. I've tried to introduce you to several very smart, eligible young men tonight. In fact," her mother said, circling her long fingers around Miranda's elbow, squeezing a little too tightly, "if you look to your right..." Her mother gave a tremendous sigh. "Subtly, Miranda, *subtly*."

"Mom, it's okay." She gently brushed her mom's hand away. "I have Dak."

Her mother watched her for a long moment, her expression becoming surprisingly tender, then resigned. "I don't want to see you get hurt, Miranda."

"I won't."

"You need someone strong."

"I know."

"Someone who can handle...you. Steven—"

"Steven wasn't kind to me. He didn't have my back. He contorted himself to please his friends."

"Why do you always assume you know what I'm going to say? Steven wasn't right for you. Nice family, but it would never have worked. You're too bull-headed."

"And that's why Dak is my man. He's strong enough to handle all that is this glorious woman that I've become. He's kind, and I love him."

She could see the worry and concern still lingering in her mother's gaze.

"He is very good-looking and successful. You'll like him."

"Yes, but you're different from your sisters. You need a

solid man. One who'll be there for you and who will let you shine."

"And they don't need that?"

Her mother gave her a meaningful look. "You *know* what I mean."

"I'm going to look for Dak." Miranda edged away from her mom, starting to worry that Dak's run-in with his ex-wife had reminded him of all the ways that love could hurt a person. Because tonight, all Miranda kept thinking about was how Jari had illustrated so many important ways that she still didn't know Dak. Such as his aversion to tuxedos. Part of tonight's dress code.

Miranda hurried across the ballroom, not even bothering to keep an eye out for Dak any longer. The man wasn't coming. She'd been stood up just like her mother feared.

He hadn't texted or called. He was making a fool out of her, and it hurt.

Landon leaned out of a conversation as she passed, asking, "You seen Dak?"

She shook her head and smiled. Her first chance to proudly parade Dak around as her boyfriend, where it didn't look as though he was being paid to be her boyfriend, and everyone noticed his absence.

On the other side of the ballroom's doors, Miranda stopped moving and breathed deeply, controlling her futile frustration. She wanted to be angry with Dak. She also wanted to shove him in her mother's face.

She wanted to scream. She should leave and find Dak and confront him for standing her up. Because two hours. Two. Hours!

Who did that? Not a man who said he loved her. Because if this was how he showed it, he wasn't enough for her.

She checked her phone, hoping there was a message saying…something. Anything. Something to prove he loved her and hadn't intended to make a fool of her.

Nothing.

Why hadn't Dak told her he hated tuxedos? Was it even true, or had Jari played her?

What if Dak had been in an accident? No, she didn't want to think tragic thoughts, she was too agitated as it was.

She eyed the doors to the ballroom, knowing she should go back in. Make further excuses for Dak. Instead, she moved toward the building's exit.

She was nearly running by the time she reached the doors, alarming the doorman, who scrambled to open one for her.

What if tonight wasn't about tuxedos or accidents? What if it was her worst fear come to life? What if she wasn't worth getting dressed up for?

Miranda stopped on the sidewalk, gulping air so she wouldn't cry.

"Ma'am?" the valet asked, hand extended for her car's ticket, his eyes wide.

She shook her head, unsure. She walked past the rows of potted trees, decorated in white lights and red ribbon bows, fighting her thoughts.

Her mother's comments were getting to her. She only needed to shrug off her doubts like she always did and carry on.

She didn't know Dak very well, but the things she knew were the most vital to a relationship.

They were good together and, because she'd felt nothing like this with anyone else, she knew it was important. More important than these stupid doubts that were trying to destroy her evening, cause her to snap at Dak and ruin every-thing when he finally appeared.

MIRANDA QUICKLY DABBED at the corner of her eye as Daisy-Mae approached.

"You okay?" Daisy-Mae asked. "I saw you leave and not come back."

Miranda gave her what she hoped was a proper smile. The woman looked amazing. Like a real-life Barbie in a glittery gown, tiny jewels in her hair, standing between the lit-up trees on the sidewalk.

"I'm okay," Miranda assured her.

"You're not," Daisy-Mae said firmly, taking in her expression. She steered them around the corner of the building where there'd be more privacy. A blast of icy wind hit their exposed arms, and they both squealed, pivoting to the spot they'd vacated, edging up to the tall heaters. "Who has you upset?"

"Nobody."

"Yeah, I used to date him. He drove my mother nuts back in high school."

Miranda took in Daisy-Mae. She was glowing with happiness. Genuine Grade A happiness. But instead of hanging out with whoever the source of that happiness was, she was here, freezing alongside Miranda.

Daisy-Mae narrowed her eyes. "Dish."

She shrugged, rubbing her cold arms. "It's fine. Really."

"You're not a very good liar. Start with your first thought," Daisy-Mae suggested. "What's got you all tangled up and freezing your butt off out here?"

Miranda's head felt swollen from holding in her tears and

self-doubts. There was no way she was going to let anyone know how she truly felt about being stood up. Because two hours late? If there'd been an accident, she would have heard about it by now. She'd been stood up.

"I was talking to my mom, that's all."

"An efficient start for a bad night, I take it?"

"Sometimes. It was weird, though. She hates my dress—"

Daisy-Mae gasped, her look one of outrage. "She's a hater?"

Miranda couldn't help but laugh. "She has…ideas. And they extend from dating to personal and professional presentation as well."

"Ah." Daisy-Mae gave her a knowing glance. "Gotcha."

"She means well, but…" She couldn't put her finger on her mother's concerns. They'd felt extra strong tonight along with a side dish of something softer, like worry. Actual, genuine worry for Miranda, and not just regarding how her life might play out through stories told by others at the club.

"She knows I want something different and that I don't want to be a trust-fund baby or some princess married to a man who feels I complete his look."

Daisy-Mae nodded. "You want to be special."

"Yes! I want to be special." That was exactly it. She wanted to be *different* from the others when it came to a man like Dak.

A sob hiccuped from within her, and she turned away, horrified.

Daisy-Mae's cool hand caressed her back, and a folded tissue appeared like magic. Miranda sniffed and dabbed at her eyes, tipping her head upward, furious at herself for crying. She had to return to the gala with her chin held high and no signs of weakness or tears, and currently she was failing.

"My mom thinks Dak isn't enough for me." A shudder

escaped her. "But I feel like he saw me!" She turned to Daisy-Mae, knowing her expression was pleading for this woman to tell her that her heart was right, not wrong.

"He respected my hot mess of a self and didn't ask me to change." Miranda leaned against the freezing marble wall behind her, watching cars go by, really hoping Dak didn't take this moment to finally show up.

She let out a sigh, suddenly spent.

"Dak accepted me. Just like this." She shrugged helplessly, surprised to see Daisy-Mae's eyes were damp.

Miranda bolted upright. "You weren't in love with him, too?" she asked, heart in her throat.

Daisy-Mae smiled, head shaking. "No, no. Not at all." Her friend reached out and gave her arm a supportive squeeze. "I can just see how special he is to you."

Miranda nodded, her eyes welling. She hated to admit it, but she had dreams about marrying this man.

"It's scary where you are right now," Daisy-Mae said sympathetically. "You could get rejected and have your heart broken. It's hard to trust your heart."

Miranda inhaled shakily. "He believes in me, and I didn't realize how important that is to me." She swiped under her eyes with the balled-up tissue. "Maybe I've let my fears freak me out because I love him so much."

Miranda felt her emotions crumbling again, and she straightened her shoulders, refusing to fall apart. She loved Dak, and the man deserved a chance to explain why he'd stood her up. He believed in her, and she needed to return the favor, no matter how difficult it was at the moment.

Daisy-Mae was shivering, and Miranda started moving them both toward the doors that led to the gala. And as she drifted inside, she whispered a prayer that she wouldn't soon look like a fool in both her love life as well as her business life.

Dak, slightly out of breath from the sprint he'd taken up the ballroom steps from the car park, realized just how nervous he was about being late. His cardio was fine, but his nerves were shot. He was over two hours late when he should have been at least thirty minutes early. He should've been one of the first to arrive, greeting guests and glad-handing each and every one of them while glued to Miranda's side.

Miranda was a reasonable woman, but this was a very important night for her, and him flaking out didn't reflect well on her. He was breaking promises. To himself. To her.

He paused in front of the ballroom doors, taking a deep breath before opening them. As soon as he stepped inside, the soft tones of a cello filled his mind. Someone slid up beside him. "Hello, Jessica Davenport from the San Antonio Sunshine News. We haven't seen you with Miranda this evening; do you have a statement for us on the status of your relationship?"

"Have you seen her?" he asked, scanning the room. The place looked amazing. It was fully decorated for the holidays with gold, red, and green. He brushed his hands down his sleeves, realizing he had a white stain on his left sleeve. Surreptitiously, he picked at it. Whipped cream. That wasn't chipping off. He needed water.

The reporter was still asking him questions, hoping for a statement. Dak backed up, planning to push the door behind him open with his back. It was a pull door. Of course.

He nodded at Jessica, whipped open the door, and headed

straight to the bathroom to fix his sleeve. He grumbled to himself the entire way.

"There you are, man. I thought the whole tuxedo-fear thing had you standing up our boss," Leo said from the sink next to Dak.

Dak just shook his head and furiously worked at the whipped cream stain.

He could feel Leo's eyes on him.

"I don't have a fear of tuxedos," Dak said finally.

"Sure looks like you do."

Dak yanked at his bowtie, trying to straighten it and making it worse. He ground his teeth together and tried to remember to breathe. There had been that meditation and visualization guy that would come into the locker room before important games. What was that breathing pattern for nerves again? Breathe in for a count of four, hold it for four, exhale for four? Or was it seven? Five? Either way, he didn't have time for that right now.

"I think Miranda's looking for you," Leo said. "Although I saw her leave a while ago."

"She left?" A spear of alarm hit Dak.

Leo shrugged. "Just so you know, rumor is your relationship is a publicity stunt."

Dak growled, grabbed a white towel from the attendant, nearly body-checking the man when he didn't step out of the way fast enough as Dak hustled from the room.

"This is one of those things where you gotta arrive on time," Leo called, tailing him. "She's an important person. And a babe. You got to treat her top rate."

Dak whirled, and whatever was showing in his expression brought Leo up short, his hands lifting to protect his face. "Just trying to be a friend, man."

"I know I messed up tonight. Find me Miranda."

Leo slowly lowered his guard.

"You see her, you let me know."

As soon as Dak got inside the ballroom, a new reporter found him.

"Have you seen Miranda Fairchild?" Dak asked before the reporter could open his mouth.

"I'm hoping to get a photo of you two together," the man said, lifting his camera. "Although what is the nature of your romantic relationship? Does it exist outside the team atmosphere?" When Dak glowered at him, he said, "You know, like a rent-a-boyfriend for Dragons' events?"

"If I were a rent-a-boyfriend, don't you think I would've been here on time?" Dak growled.

"Sure, but an actual boyfriend would've also been here on time. So I'm confused."

"Well, it doesn't matter if you're confused or not. I'm her boyfriend," Dak said, pushing past him. "End of story."

"The ten thousand people who read my articles care if I get it right!"

Dak barely held in a string of swears. He'd forgotten about this part of fame and how any small misstep was gossip-worthy and could make a touchy situation—such as publicly standing up your new girlfriend—so much worse.

He saw a woman with dark hair, and before he realized she wasn't nearly curvy enough, he had already grasped her elbow and said hello.

Realizing his mistake, he gave her a quick nod and wished the stranger a good time at the gala and kept moving. He didn't even know what color dress he was looking for.

He saw Maverick by the bar, alone. "Have you seen Miranda?"

"Not recently."

"What's she wearing?"

Maverick scratched his jaw. "I don't know. Something designer, probably."

"What color?" Dak snapped impatiently. The room was filled, the gala obviously a success.

"Red maybe? Why don't you call her?"

Dak whipped out his phone, cursing his panic for forgetting he had a way of contacting her. There was a long string of text messages from her that had ended about half an hour ago. His call went to voicemail.

"Hey, don't you have to give a speech?" Maverick asked.

"Miranda, I'm here," Dak said, leaving his message. "I can't find you. Call me." He made sure his ringer was on as loud as it would go and pocketed his phone.

"They were looking for you a few minutes ago." Maverick pointed toward the stage.

What?

"Right," Dak said. He checked his watch. He was late for that too, and had forgotten his speech cards in the car.

"You okay?"

"Sure. But I really wish I had a time machine. Or a clone."

He hurried to the stage, knowing that even though he was here now, he had messed up with the woman he loved. And to make it even worse, on one of the most important nights of her year.

And that was pretty unforgivable.

MIRANDA RETURNED TO THE BALLROOM, figuring if she ditched her own charity event it would look even worse than Dak being a no-show.

A reporter sidled up to her. "Jessica Davenport from the San Antonio Sunshine News."

"Yes, we met earlier." Miranda pretended to take a sip of her wine but, realizing her hand was shaking, lowered it again.

"Would you care to comment on what it's like to date a former NHL star? As a civilian, a woman, an owner who has admitted she doesn't know much about the sport, does it feel as though you've bought him as the fulfillment of a fantasy?"

Miranda crossed her free arm across her chest, keeping a tight grip on her wine so it didn't accidentally wind up all over the reporter.

She paused a beat, double-checking her reaction, then asked. "Are you serious?"

Jessica blinked, politely waiting for her to comment.

"Do you think that me pouring my inheritance into a team and trying to do right by these players, trying to help my community and families with sick kids, looks like a woman acting out a fantasy about having an athlete on her arm? Do you realize how ridiculous you sound?" Her voice had grown loud enough to be heard over the cello playing softly in the corner, and necks were craning to hear what the fuss was about. "That might be how some misguided men in power think and behave, but maybe you need to learn a bit more about women. About me. Your question disgusts me."

She turned on her heel and marched a few steps away before realizing everyone had stopped what they were doing. The cello had gone silent, and people were giving her cautious looks.

On stage, someone spoke into the microphone, and slowly everyone turned their attention his way. As the auction announcements got underway, Miranda stood, clapping, smiling and being that polite and lovely woman everyone wanted while on the inside she was positively fuming.

Was it obvious to everyone that, despite her wealth and success, Dak was out of her league? And why were they so intent on pointing it out to her tonight? Everyone except Daisy-Mae, who'd done a darn good job of putting her back together again.

As the announcements went on, Miranda's cheeks hurt from her wide, fake smile, and her glass of wine rested heavily in her hand. She clapped on cue and allowed herself to get lost in the room's white noise surrounding her.

She just wanted to go home.

She wanted to go to Sweetheart Creek, curl up on her couch in her yoga pants, and try to coax Captain, the stray cat she'd been feeding, to come through the cat door Dak had installed for him.

Most of all, she wanted to be far away from here when they called Dak on stage and discovered he hadn't shown up.

Further embarrassment. Her mom was right. She'd hired someone unreliable.

Dated someone who didn't make commitments a priority.

A small voice in the back of her head reminded her that there could still be a reasonable explanation. An emergency. A crisis.

But Dak had admitted he rushed into things and made mistakes. Look at his café. He loved it, but not enough. He had loved Jari, but not enough. Who was to say she was any different? He was that special kind of man that made everybody think they were special too, when in reality they were that same forgettable person they'd always been.

She tuned out the speech, politely clapping when others did, until a familiar rich, warm voice filled the room. Her head snapped up, and she locked eyes with Dak. He'd found her among the hundreds of people and was staring at her from the stage. Her heart thumped.

He was here.

She mattered.

Or maybe the obligation of his job mattered. He hadn't found her all evening or answered her texts, after all.

Stop it. She was her own worst enemy, her mom's fears becoming her own. She *knew* Dak.

There was a valid reason she hadn't seen him yet tonight.

He finished his speech, and she realized she hadn't heard a word. She watched him move confidently down the stairs, his head of dark hair moving across the room, weaving between people. He was heading her way. She faltered. She didn't know what to do, what to say when she saw him. What if they made a scene? What if he dumped her in front of everyone, like Steven had at that awful fundraiser gala two years ago?

She froze, debating which way to run when Dak appeared at her side.

"I'm sorry I'm late. Really late." His expression was full of worry, regret, and something worse as he waited for her to answer.

She nodded and gave him a fake, bright smile that hurt. "Sure, we'll talk later. I know there are a lot of people who want to take a photo of you." She gestured to the reporters that had clustered, cameras raised, shutters already clicking.

The scent of fresh gingerbread wafted off Dak, sending her a wave of homesickness, a longing for what could have been. He leaned close, hand on her elbow as he smiled for a camera. "Really, I'm sorry. The café went insane. I zipped in to take care of one thing and left my phone in the car because I was thinking if I did—"

"Here. Smile," Miranda said, turning him to face the camera, hiding behind him for a moment, collecting herself, willing back the tears pushing for release in the face of his excuses. Yes, they were likely legit, but she just couldn't handle his café being his excuse right now. How was someone's latte more important than her?

"That's all for now, thank you," Miranda said once she'd also smiled for the cameras, letting Dak's arm drape over her shoulder like they were a happy couple.

She began walking away and was halfway across the ballroom when she realized Dak had fallen behind. She looked over her shoulder and he stretched out his hand.

He took two steps forward, still reaching for her.

"What are you doing?" she asked, taking in the smiling faces of people surrounding them, hoping to see something magical and romantic happen.

Dak tangled her fingers in his, his smile kind even though uncertain. For a moment, she thought he was going to whisk her away to Sweetheart Creek. Instead, he pulled her onto the dance floor, his arm going around her waist, holding her like she belonged.

"I promised you a dance," he whispered.

"I thought you hated tuxedos."

"I do. With a passion." He reached up and yanked at the bow tie that was crooked and twisted as though he'd been yanking on it for hours. The jacket sleeve was damp where it was touching her wrist. The man appeared to be a walking disaster. But he was here, in a tux.

For her.

"You really didn't go to things with Jari if you had to wear a tux?"

Dak swallowed. "I..." He sighed. "No."

"Why me?"

He met her gaze. "You're worth it."

Oh.

Her heart lifted, the forming ice around it beginning to melt.

"My parents arrived an hour ago," he said, halfway through the song. "They'd like to meet you tomorrow."

"What? Where are they?" Miranda asked.

"Trying to save the café's night. I told them to kick everyone out because I had somewhere to be, and that I was already unforgivably late."

"You didn't."

He gently cradled her chin, lifting it so he could meet her gaze. It was all she could do to not look away. "I promise I will never be late like this ever again."

"How can you promise something like that?" she asked, hating how her voice broke.

"Tonight I let myself get swept up in the crap life throws at me. I've got to let my staff struggle, fail, and ultimately take more responsibility. I know where my priorities are. I messed up tonight, but I won't again."

He looked down, and with the seriousness of his gaze, the warmth of his love, she felt a soaring hope.

"Please, will you meet my parents?"

It was all so fast, but it all felt so right. All she could do was nod and say, "I'd love to."

ak hadn't expected Miranda to be so nervous about meeting his parents. He'd met her parents at last night's gala, and that had been an...interesting experience. Mrs. Fairchild's cool, polite reserve had only served to remind him how much he loved Miranda's energy, warmth and enthusiasm.

He'd met Mr. Fairchild as well. The man had given him a quick handshake, looked him up and down, nodded to his daughter and then excused himself to undoubtably speak to people "more important" than his daughter and her date.

The coolness of that meeting had made the event of introducing Miranda to his parents feel all the more weighty and important. He wanted them to accept her and invite her into the Morisette family fold—a place he was sure she'd belong. Even more so than within her own family.

But Miranda was jittery, as though uncertain about the timing of meeting each other's family when she still had doubts and the fears about him, and his level of commitment to her.

Seeing those doubts last night had hurt. Hurt worse than his shoulder after it had been torn apart.

But Miranda meeting his parents felt like the natural next step, and he hoped it helped her realize how important she was to him.

They were in his condo, his new puppy in her kennel as she refused to stop licking Miranda. In the corner, Dak's Christmas tree twinkled merrily. Miranda was sitting beside him on the couch in a fitted dress, her knees together and angled to the side, hands clasped in her lap. Across from them his parents sat on a separate couch with Milo sprawled between them, belly up to receive a stomach rub from Dak's dad.

"So I hear you're the owner of the Dragons," his dad said to Miranda, and Dak could have sworn he heard the shot of a starting pistol. Game on.

"Yes."

His father continued to drill Miranda about the NHL, her team's division, her players and even some strategies. She had answers for just about everything, and the things she kept silent about were either trade secrets or up to the coaches.

Dak's mom kept elbowing his dad and rolling her eyes apologetically at Miranda. But Miranda stayed focused on Eddie, as though knowing how important his approval was.

"I hope you're keeping our boy in line," his dad said finally, apparently out of hockey questions.

"I think it's the other way around," she quipped, and Dak smiled, squeezing her hand.

"So you're a person he needs to keep in line?" his dad asked with a scowl. Dak sent him a warning look.

"Completely," Miranda said with a straight face. "He brings

out the competition in me. I plan to break all of his records. The ones that aren't on the ice, that is. I don't skate."

"Do you plan to learn? Hockey is a big part of my son's life."

"Owning an NHL team isn't being involved enough?" she challenged.

"He doesn't play any longer. Nothing but shinny. You gonna pick up skates and play?"

She turned to Dak. "Do you want me to?"

"I don't know, you're pretty competitive. I might get you into some trouble if you're trying to keep up with me."

"That's it," she said firmly, picking up her phone.

"What are you doing? Calling a ride?" his dad asked with a smug smile.

Dak's heart raced as he tried to think of a way to keep Miranda from leaving. His dad was difficult, but he didn't mean anything by it.

"No, I'm booking private skating lessons to bring me up to speed." She gave Eddie a satisfied smile over the top of her phone.

His dad stared at her for a long moment, and Dak and his mother shared a panicked look. Then his dad let out the loudest belly laugh Dak had ever heard. Miranda just smiled. His dad wagged a finger at Miranda and shook his head. "You're a real keeper, aren't you?"

"I'm the only female owner in the NHL. It's going to take a little more than a game of twenty questions to run me off."

"Yes, you'll do just fine." He got up, clapping Dak on the shoulder. But Dak couldn't look away from the only woman who'd ever battled his dad and won—other than his mother.

"You'd better put a ring on her finger and lock her in. You're never gonna find another one like Miranda."

"Well, I do have a thought about doing that, but I have a feeling she'll tell me I'm moving too fast."

"No such thing when it all feels right," his father replied, heading to the kitchen.

Miranda turned to Dak's mom, her expression somber. "You were at the café last night? I hear it was busy?"

His mother gasped and spun on Dak. "Did you not get there at all?"

"I got there! I was late, though. *Really* late."

Amara turned to Miranda with sympathy. "He left you hanging, didn't he? And I bet you looked so beautiful and put so much work into your appearance." His mom darted a furious glance at Dak and shook her head. "Mr. Latey-Pants." She clucked her tongue.

"The café was busy?" Miranda asked again. She wouldn't look at Dak, staying focused on his mother.

"It was a zoo. He suggested we kick everyone out and close the doors so he could get to the gala."

Miranda looked at Dak with an expression he couldn't read. His left leg started jiggling, and he swallowed hard. He had a feeling Miranda was coming to a very important decision right now.

"His sense of duty is very strong," his mom said. "It's one of the things I admire about him, but sometimes this man takes on too much. That café was bursting at the seams. We pitched in, but I'm afraid we didn't arrive early enough to avoid his tardiness. I hope your evening turned out okay."

Her sincerity was so genuine, Miranda's chin trembled. Again, this woman belonged with the Morisette's. They were a crazy mess of chaos sometimes, but they cared for each other.

"I understand crazy zoos," Miranda said, her voice strong.

"But this man needs to learn to send text messages." She gave him a firm look. "One voicemail after arriving two hours late isn't nearly enough."

Dak winced. "I know." He wasn't sure how to make things right again. He knew the press had hounded her all night, and it was because of him. This was exactly why she hadn't wanted to date him, because things could backfire on her and she already had so much being fired at her. He had made her life more difficult last night.

Warm fingers slipped between his own. "But I also know he's a good man who would never intentionally hurt me," Miranda said.

And when Dak looked up, all he saw was a woman with love shining from her eyes. And he knew everything between himself and Miranda was going to be okay.

MIRANDA KNEW it was going to happen even before Dak's mom gasped, or before Dak got down on one knee.

Everything was moving so fast.

They'd only known each other for two months, and yet it already felt so right, so certain. There was still so much to learn about each other, and yet, there was a connection beneath the details, where she knew who Dak was at his core. And that was all that mattered. She was loved.

"Miranda Fairchild, you are the most competitive woman I have ever met. You're crazy and bold. You're willing to take on things that nobody in their right mind would. And somehow you make it work. And so," Dak said, revealing a velvet ring box, "I can't help but think that if you're boldly willing to take on all that is crazy and make it work, that maybe you would take me on as your husband. I promise to love you, and to kick everyone out of my café when you need me."

When it truly mattered, he'd been there. The gala was… Miranda thought back to her insecurities from the night before. Most of them had been her taking on someone else's fears, and they hadn't truly been her own. Well, they had, but they were those discontinued, still-in-stock doubts, those last-ditch attempts at self-preservation before she could fall the rest of the way in love, before she could fully trust her heart.

Galas had never brought out the best in her, but the results were always good. They'd raised an incredible amount of money for families in need last night.

"You were drop-dead gorgeous in that velvet dress last night," Dak said. "You took my breath away."

"Nice of you to finally compliment me," she teased.

"I was too busy groveling. But know that I think you're a hottie, both on the inside and the outside. You have intelligence and courage, and even when people are unkind to you, you return nothing but kindness. I don't know how you do it."

Tears streamed down Miranda's cheeks, his words bursting open the internal box where she stuffed it all. He pulled her into his arms, holding her tight.

"I don't hold it together," she admitted. "I'm actually a hottie of a mess who's ruining your proposal."

DAK CLOSED HIS EYES. It was too soon to propose. Wouldn't he ever learn?

He didn't even know Miranda had these hidden insecurities. He only saw the courage. He saw the vulnerability, yes, but not the pain that came with it.

He cursed himself for being so late last night. And yet, he

felt as though by messing up, he'd allowed himself a new window to see into the woman he loved. He wanted to protect her, shelter her, to be the wall to lean against when she was exhausted from holding herself up.

He tilted her face upward so he could catch her expression, figure out what she was feeling.

"I think you're beautiful and strong. Real and human." The tears kept streaking. "My proposal is genuine. The offer is open for as long as you need." He gently kissed her forehead, repeating himself. "For as long as you need."

"How do you know?" she asked, her voice choked. "You've been here before. How do you know we're meant to be, and that it'll all work out?"

Dak steadied his gaze, then slowly lifted a fist to his chest. "Because I feel it. Right here. Unwavering, unquestionable certainty."

He was quoting her from when she'd told him how she carried on with her team in the face of opposition and public doubt.

He received a soft smile of acknowledgment, her shoulders relaxing.

"I've felt that since the first moment you sat down across that long slab of maple and smiled at me. I love you, Miranda Fairchild. Will you please consider marrying me?"

Say yes, say yes, Dak chanted inside his head.

He'd never been so nervous in all his life. Not even waiting to see if he'd been drafted into the NHL.

He knew he'd told her he'd wait. And he would.

Even though it was maybe too soon, he felt it in his bones. Then seeing Miranda and his dad spar, and the fact that she probably had indeed booked herself private skating lessons, had sealed the deal. He didn't have to look any further, and he didn't have to wait any longer.

He knew. Right here. Right now.

Miranda Fairchild was the woman for him.

All she had to do was say yes.

Or at least give him some sign that she'd heard him.

He knew he needed to be patient, to give her time. Whatever decision she came to would be the one she stuck to. But he really needed to know. If yes, start planning. If no, he'd just work harder to prove to her he was the one for her.

"Miranda?"

She looked at him, her expression hinting that she already had an answer. She just needed the courage to speak it out loud.

He vowed to remain quiet, to let her speak when she was ready.

At the edge of the room, he could feel his parents hovering, waiting, listening, hoping as much as he was. They had only just met her, but he knew she had their seal of approval.

Finally, Miranda looked up at him through her long lashes. And then she said the sweetest word he'd ever heard.

"Yes."

EPILOGUE

Miranda hustled down the corridor from the VIP box where she'd viewed most of the game. The Dragons had won minutes ago, the arena oddly quieting for a few moments after she left the box before the roar took up again. The PR team had obviously done something down there that hadn't been on the New Year's Eve PR plan. But judging from the noise, it was good.

Checking her watch, Miranda lengthened her strides. She needed to get to the press room to provide a few soundbites.

Jeremy grabbed her arm. "Did you hear?"

"I'm sorry, I've got quotes to give in the press room. Walk and talk?"

He fell into step beside her.

What was he doing here anyway? He rarely ever came to games, and she hadn't seen him in the VIP box with her, Dak, and a few others.

The arena was going wild with noise again, and she bit her bottom lip. The PR team had severely veered from the plan, which meant the reporters would be later getting to the press room, which meant she'd be late for rendezvousing with Dak outside the stadium.

She'd never hear the end of it if she wasn't on time for their elopement. He'd think she'd developed cold feet. And that would be worse than him arriving late for the gala. Much worse.

"Maverick just got engaged."

Miranda came to a full stop. "What? When?"

Her mind ran through the various scenarios on what this could mean in the press. Good things? Bad things? Was this even real? Or was this all part of that crazy plan the publicity team had concocted? He wasn't seeing anyone as far as she knew. He'd been chummy with Daisy-Mae, who obviously had a crush on him, but refused to ask him out. Oh, the poor woman would be so disappointed when she heard the news.

Miranda grumbled to herself and paced one way, then the other. Indecision weighed on her. She needed to check on Daisy-Mae. She also needed to get some quotes to the press room.

"Is his engagement public?"

Jeremy grinned. "You could say that."

"Okay. Do we have a statement for the press? They might ask me about it."

"I'm sure they will."

The PR team was going to want to weigh in on this before she said anything. They'd been working on Maverick's reputation all season. It desperately needed mending, and something like this could really, really help him.

Dak. Dak was waiting for her in a limo, ready to whisk her away.

Miranda circled back to Jeremy, facing him again. Because, really, when it came right down to it, she only needed to know one thing.

"Who did Maverick propose to?"

ACKNOWLEDGMENTS

To Ted Lasso's Rebecca. While writing this story she was the original Slays All Day babe who can rock any outfit, be vulnerable, strong, lovable and basically be the kind of woman I want to be when I grow up.

Super big hugs to my HEA team. I adore you. Thank you for your love, support, and nitpicks. Lots of love!

GET THE HOT GOSSIP

Do you want the story behind the story? Read all the juicy gossip on Jean's characters, which real life NHLers and movie stars inspired the characters in The Gingerbread Cafe, enjoy extended and deleted scenes and much more.

Read it all at:
www.jeanoram.com/gingerbreadbonus

HOCKEY SWEETHEARTS

Have you read them all?

The Cupcake Cottage

Peach Blossom Hollow

Chocolate Cherry Cabin

The Peppermint Lodge

The Huckleberry Bookshop

Sugar Cookie Country House

The Gingerbread Cafe

A Tiny House Christmas

There are more stories set in Sweetheart Creek, Texas in these two series:

The Cowboys of Sweetheart Creek, Texas

The Cowboy's Stolen Heart (Levi)

The Cowboy's Secret Wish (Myles)

The Cowboy's Second Chance (Ryan)

The Cowboy's Sweet Elopement (Brant)

The Cowboy's Surprise Return (Cole)

MORE SMALL TOWN ROMANCES BY JEAN ORAM…

Veils and Vows

The Promise (Book 0: Devon & Olivia)

The Surprise Wedding (Book 1: Devon & Olivia)

A Pinch of Commitment (Book 2: Ethan & Lily)

The Wedding Plan (Book 3: Luke & Emma)

Accidentally Married (Book 4: Burke & Jill)

The Marriage Pledge (Book 5: Moe & Amy)

Mail Order Soulmate (Book 6: Zach & Catherine)

Blueberry Springs

Whiskey and Gumdrops (Mandy & Frankie)

Rum and Raindrops (Jen & Rob)

Eggnog and Candy Canes (Katie & Nash)

Sweet Treats (3 short stories—Mandy, Amber, & Nicola)

Vodka and Chocolate Drops (Amber & Scott)

Tequila and Candy Drops (Nicola & Todd)

Champagne and Lemon Drops (Beth & Oz)

The Summer Sisters

Falling for the Movie Star

Falling for the Boss

Falling for the Single Dad

Falling for the Bodyguard

Falling for the Firefighter

MORE SMALL TOWN ROMANCES BY JEAN ORAM...

Fairy Godmothers and Other Fiascos

Fairy Godmothers Aren't Cheap

Run, Run Rudolph

The Problem with Cupid

Indigo Bay

Sweet Matchmaker (Ginger and Logan)

Sweet Holiday Surprise (Cash & Alexa)

Sweet Forgiveness (Ashton & Zoe)

Sweet Troublemaker (Nick & Polly)

Sweet Joymaker (Maria & Clint)

ABOUT THE AUTHOR

Jean Oram is a *New York Times* and *USA Today* bestselling romance author. Inspiration for her small town series came from her own upbringing on the Canadian prairies. Although, so far, none of her characters have grown up in an old schoolhouse or worked on a bee farm. Jean still lives on the prairie with her husband, two kids, and big shaggy dog where she can be found out playing in the snow or hiking.

Become an Official Fan:
www.facebook.com/groups/jeanoramfans
Instagram: www.instagram.com/author_jeanoram
Facebook: www.facebook.com/JeanOramAuthor
Shop: shop.jeanoram.com
Newsletter: www.jeanoram.com/signup
Website & blog: www.jeanoram.com